# BEAR GULCH

## McCain Cronicles
### Book Three

## B.N. Rundell

WOLFPACK
PUBLISHING
— EST 2013 —

**Bear Gulch**
Paperback Edition
Copyright © 2023 B.N. Rundell

Wolfpack Publishing
9850 S. Maryland Parkway, Suite A-5 #323
Las Vegas, Nevada 89183

wolfpackpublishing.com

Paperback ISBN 978-1-63977-806-5
eBook ISBN 978-1-63977-807-2
LCCN 2023937185

# Preface

Historical fiction, kind of a misnomer. If it's historical, it should be accurate and truthful. If it's fiction, that means it's not the truth, but the imagination of the author. So, historical fiction is actually true to life. Have you not had times that your life was truthful, but there were a few fringes that weren't quite known or revealed to others, secrets maybe, something that only you knew and did not tell? So it is with historical fiction—I do my best to ensure my stories are historically accurate. Accurate as to the general happenings and gear etc., and even to the including of some actual characters and events such as those used in this story. But it's up to you, the reader, to determine which parts, characters, happenings are historical, and which are fiction. I'm grinning as I write these words, knowing the consternation that might bring to the minds of some. But, just smile, laugh maybe, and hopefully enjoy. You're not just the reader, you are, in your own way, a character in the story as you ride along with the characters, look at the scenery, and become a part. So, enjoy yourself, my friend, and may we meet again soon, perhaps somewhere in the past.

# BEAR GULCH

# CHAPTER 1

## BOZEMAN

The rattle of gunfire brought Eli from his blankets like a hungry trout jumping for a mayfly. With rifle in hand he searched the moonlit darkness for attackers, saw nothing, glanced to his horses who stood with heads lifted, ears pricked, looking beyond the camp to the ridge that paralleled the valley below. He had been traveling south from Helena for more than a week, searching for his runaway boys, twins Jubal and Joshua Paine, who had last been seen chasing the elusive gold nymph. His search began in Louisville, the home of his wife's family, where prior to her death, he promised he would find the boys, deserters from the Union Army, and bring them home. He lost their sign after leaving Jefferson City in Montana Territory and taking the well-traveled road that sided the Boulder River. Although he had word they might go to Confederate Gulch, a more promising lead pointed him south toward the Bozeman Trail and the Alder Gulch area, but that had been most of a week past.

Now he was about halfway to Virginia City and was

camped high up a hill that overlooked the Bozeman Trail, the route that had brought the thousands of gold seekers and settlers through Indian country contrary to the Laramie Peace Treaty of 1851. It was that tide of white men that rankled the natives, especially Red Cloud, the war leader of the Oglala Sioux nation. The Sioux had allied with the Northern Arapaho and the Northern Cheyenne, and the three nations had launched a war against the many incursions into their lands and the slaughter of the buffalo herds that were their mainstay of life.

Eli looked about, sat down, and shook his boots free of any critters that might have made their beds in the warm dark hovel, and slipped them on. He grabbed up his jacket, and with rifle in hand walked to the crest of the ridge just above his camp. The rattle of gunfire had subsided to a few sporadic shots, and Eli dropped to his haunches to look into the wide valley below. The moon was waxing toward full, but a few clouds masked its light, yet Eli could see the silvery ribbon of the little creek that came from the mountains behind him and fed the Madison River. The Bozeman Trail sided the Madison for a bit before cutting through the rolling hills and turning south toward Virginia City and Alder Gulch.

It was in that bottom flat that Eli saw fires blossom, giving light to the shadowy figures, most on horseback, others sprawled in the grass beside wagons that were flaring up with flames that licked at the darkness. The rifles were silenced but screamed war cries could be heard no louder than the squeal of a mouse. The wagons were just shy of a mile away and Eli counted at least a dozen. That would mean if they were all gold hunters, probably thirty to fifty men, but if it was families, no more than twenty men; the others would be women and children. Eli shook his head as the smell of smoke drifted toward him, sliding up the slope of the ridge where he now sat. The smell of burning flesh made him cover his nose and mouth with his neckerchief as he shook his head at the foolishness of so many of these people that continued to flood into Indian country, even against the counsel of the military and common sense.

He turned his back on the carnage, walked back over the ridge to his camp, and began saddling his horse and rigging his packhorse. He rode a long-legged claybank stallion, what some would call a lineback red dun, that was a crossbreed of Tennessee Walker and Morgan, a fine horse that came from the breeding stock of the family of his wife who were known for their fine horses in Louis-ville, Kentucky. His packhorse was a dapple-grey moun-tain-bred mustang that he had since before the war. He was a gift from a friend, Half Yellow Face, an Absáalooke scout for the army at Fort Laramie. A man he befriended while he was stationed there after his graduation from West Point and before he was transferred to Sheridan's cavalry in the war.

Although the grey appeared to be little when he stood beside the claybank, he stood just shy of fifteen hands and was solidly built. Eli had used him as his preferred mount until he left him at the family farm in Louisville during the war. Eli was a big man, six foot three inches, two hundred fifteen pounds, broad shouldered, tapered at the waist and hips, and considered by most women to be a handsome man. But with his size and weight, Eli rode Rusty, the claybank stallion that was sixteen hands, broad chested, big muscled rump, and soft eyes.

Eli had a Winchester '66 in .44 caliber in the scabbard under his right leg. A Colt 1860 Army .44 sat in the holster on his left hip, butt forward and a Bowie knife

was in a sheath on his right hip. Unseen by others, he
also had a LeMat nine-shot .44-caliber pistol tucked in
his belt at the small of his back and a Spencer .52 and
Colt revolver shotgun in the packs on the grey.

He stepped in the stirrup and swung aboard the big
stallion, pointed him to the south to drop off the ridge
behind the southern point and down the shoulder, still
hidden from view, to the coulee that carried a little creek
that would take them into the open valley. As they rode
the shoulder of the hills above the creek, the eastern sky
was showing the fading line of pale blue with pinks
rising above and painting the bellies of the few clouds
that hung lazily in the eastern sky.

Eli slipped the Winchester Yellowboy from the scabbard and lay it across the pommel, a round in the
chamber but the hammer down under his thumb. The
hillside shoulder rounded back to the north above the
meandering creek that chuckled over the rocks behind
the willows, making its way north to join the other
creeks that would eventually merge with the Madison
River. The Bozeman Trail rode the shoulders of the hills
to Eli's right, pointing to the south as Eli rode with the
current of the creek, nearing the smoldering hulks of the
wagons.

The horses had been stripped of their harnesses and
taken by the raiders along with all the rifles, pistols, and
whatever resembled or could be made into a weapon.
Bodies were strewn about, most stripped of any clothing,
scalped and mutilated. The blood and gore had already
begun to attract the carrion eaters and Eli watched
coyotes, badgers, ravens, magpies, whiskey jacks, turkey
buzzards and eagles begin to congregate, tearing at the
unburnt flesh, fighting one another for any scraps. He
rode through the wagons, his neckerchief on his face to

mask the stench of death and burned flesh, and saw nothing salvageable or living. It appeared this had been a wagon train of both families of settlers and gold-hunting men. Eli counted twenty-one men, four women, two children among the dead.

Eli drew away from the wagons, stood in his stirrups, and looked around at the hills and flats, searching for a possible burial place. He spotted a bit of a rise with a rock formation near the crest, a sharp drop-off at its shoulder that stood above a dry gulch. The white soil about was loose and soft and he reckoned this spot would do well. He shrugged, shook his head, and stepped down. He used his rawhide riata that hung coiled at the side of his pommel, grabbed another length of rope from the packs on the grey and laid them aside. Stripping the packs from the grey, and the saddlebags and bedroll from Rusty, he led the animals back to the first wagon and began the task that lay before him.

After dragging and packing all the bodies to the chosen site, stacking them under the overhang, he climbed the crest of the little knoll and began pushing the rocks off to bury the bodies. When he finished, he led the horses to the creek, found a break in the willows and looked around, stripped down to the buff and splashed into the water with a bar of lye soap in hand. The horses stood side by side, upstream of the deep water at the dogleg bend in the creek where Eli splashed about, and watched the antics of the man as he did his best to rid himself of the stench. When his body was clean, he grabbed the clothes and sat on a warm rock in the sun, bending down to scrub the clothes, rinse them clean, and spread them out on the rocks to dry as he stretched out on the big warm rock to soak up the warm sun. He was quite a sight, clothes scattered about, him naked as a newborn with a rifle at his side and staring up to the blue sky arched overhead.

With the bodies buried, most of the carrion eaters had left the scene of the carnage, but one fox still wandered about, searching and sniffing for anything that might be worth sampling. When the red-tailed canine turned and ran lickety-split, Eli rose up, rifle in hand, and looked to the horses that had been grazing on the grass nearby. Both had lifted their heads and pricked their ears forward, nostrils flaring as the willows parted to reveal a small figure in the shadow. Eli turned to face the willows, rifle at his shoulder, and called, "Come outta there whoever you are!"

"Wait, mister, don't shoot!" called a voice that sounded quite young.

Eli grabbed his britches and lay them over his lap, "Come out where I can see you!" he ordered.

"But if we do, we can see you, too!" giggled the voice that Eli was certain was that of a girl.

"Alright, alright. Hold on there, let me get some clothes on." He chuckled as he grabbed at the rest of his clothes and scampered into them. As he slipped on his boots, he said, "Alright, you can come out now."

He sat with the rifle across his legs as he watched the willows shake. A young woman came from the brush, followed by two youngsters, a boy and a girl, the girl about ten and the boy about six. He guessed the young woman to be about fifteen or sixteen. As they stood on the bank looking at Eli, he stood, "So, I take it you were with the wagons?"

"Yessir. Our pa made me take the young'uns and the mule and hide out here in the bushes. He gave me a pistol so we wouldn't be taken, you know...and there was so much noise an' such, we hid under the willows and had Meg," she motioned back to the thicker brush, "lay down like she was wont to do back on the farm." She sighed heavily, looked at Eli and in a softer voice said, "I watched what you done and figgered you to be a good man."

Eli glanced back to the horses and looked at the youngsters, "You hungry?"

The boy nodded and all three said in unison, "Yessir!" The older girl adding, "We haven't eaten since breakfast yesterday."

"Then, get your mule and come on across the creek here, and we'll get us a fire goin' and get somethin' to eat. That sound alright with you?"

"Yessir!" chimed three grinning youngsters.

# CHAPTER 2

## QUESTIONS

The alder stood tall as the willows grew thick, both providing cover for the group gathered at creekside to make a meal. Eli had fetched cornmeal, flour, and his treasured section of honey that was wrapped in canvas and carried at the top of the pannier. He walked to the little fire with foodstuffs and more in hand, dropped on his haunches near the fire and began preparing the meal. With one pan for mixing, the frying pan warming on the fire and cooking a piece of fat from the pork belly, he had to set aside his work for the most important coffee. The youngsters sat watching, when the oldest, Christine, offered, "I can help with that. You're making johnnycakes, aren't you?"

"Yes, that's what I was thinking would be best, but if you've done it," he handed the pan with the beginnings of the johnnycakes, "have at it!" He grinned as he turned to his coffee making. Christine soon had the mix made, pulled the frying pan with the sizzling fat back from the flames and after picking out the rind of the pork belly, she began dropping spoonfuls of the mix into the hot grease. She looked to her siblings, "Narcissa, would you be for getting the plates and such?"

The girl nodded, pulled away from the boy, Jackson, leaving him sitting cross-legged in the grass. She went to the packs, looked back to Eli with a question, but when he nodded, she dug in the pannier and brought out three tin plates, looked around for more and looked at Eli with a question on her face. He nodded, smiling, "That's all I have. You'll just have to make do."

Narcissa nodded, and with plates in hand, walked to where Christine waited and sat the plates on the ground beside her, turned away and returned to Jackson's side, putting her arm around him as they waited. Christine looked to Eli, "The cakes are ready," as she pulled the frying pan back from the coals and began putting two johnnycakes into each of two plates, replaced the pan on the rock, and motioned for Narcissa to come get the plates.

Eli moved closer, unfolded the canvas from the section of honeycomb, and with the blade of his knife, scooped up some honey to put on the cakes, then said, "Let's have a short prayer of thanks for our food, alright?" He looked from one to the other of the three, then doffed his hat and said a short prayer of thanks for their safety, their meal, and their time together. When he said, "Amen," he looked up at three tear-stained faces and nodded to Narcissa to take the plates. She was wide-eyed when she saw the honey and hurried to Jackson, "We got honey on the cakes!" she declared, handing the boy a plate. They sat side by side, picking up the cakes with their fingers, licking their fingers clean after each one, and quickly devoured the delight.

Christine made two more pans full which allowed each one three tasty cakes with honey. When they finished, Eli said to the youngsters, "You might need to go to the creek and wash up a mite. I think you have honey from your nose to your toes!" he chuckled.

The youngsters looked at one another, then to Eli, and Jackson, with a very serious expression on his face, said, "Unnhnn, no we don't!" But Christine looked side-long at the two younger ones, one eyebrow raised, and said, "We all need to wash!" and rose as she motioned for the two to follow.

With the face-washing complete, Christine assigned cleanup tasks to each one, Eli and herself included. As they worked, Eli asked, "So, where was the wagon train going?"

Christine took a deep breath, and began, "The train was bound for Virginia City. We were going to Nevada City where my mother's brother has a livery and black-smith shop. My father was going to partner with him and make mining equipment and more."

"And where were you coming from?" asked Eli, busy at packing the panniers and doing his best to make his questioning as casual as possible. He had watched the youngsters and they were showing remarkable control over their emotions, but he thought that could not last.

"We lived in Philadelphia. Our father worked in a large shop there, making all sorts of metal things."

"And your last name?"

Christine smiled, "And is it our heritage ye be askin' a'boot?" emphasizing the Irish brogue that had not been a part of her speaking before.

Eli grinned, "So, it's Irish ye are then?!" chuckling. "I already had that pegged, what with your red hair and freckles. I have a wee bit of the Irish in me as well," he grinned as he turned about to face the three.

"Aye, our family be the Dohertys, and we hail from

county Donegal. But the three of us were born in Philadelphia! And if our mother heard me speaking with the brogue, she would be upset, for she coaxed and coached us all to rid ourselves of the brogue. Seein' as how so many looked down upon the Irish."

"Those that would do such a thing are not the kind to be concerned about. Those same ones would try to make themselves out to be superior to everyone that might be different than themselves. But you're in America now, and even though that still happens, all too often I'm ashamed to admit, the rest of us are doing our best to rid those ways from our lives and homes." He dropped to his heels as he looked at the three, now on eye level with them, "What you've been through is a terrible thing, but it was not because you're Irish. The Natives that attacked you were probably the Sioux who are fighting to keep their lands and their way of life. They lived here for centuries before the white man came, and now the white men are killing the buffalo and leaving them to waste, and taking land that is not theirs only because they lust for the riches of gold." He paused as he looked at the three, "Wherever you are, you will find there are those that want to take from others, and there will be those that seek to help others. And it's up to you which you will become. But always remember the sacrifice your Mom and Dad made so you could have a better life. Let that be your example to follow, no matter what comes your way."

He stood, looked at Christine, "So, since you were already going to Nevada City to be with your uncle, I reckon that's where we ought to go. Would that be alright with you three?" he asked, looking from one to the other, and receiving nods from each one.

The girls rode bareback on the mule, Jackson sat on

Eli's bedroll behind the cantle of his saddle, and they rode south out of the valley of bad memories. No one looked back. The sun hung in the hazy sky off their right shoulder and the hills began pushing in on the little creeks that came from the higher country. Two creeks had merged at the south end of the long valley, but the Bozeman Trail followed the larger of the two that they would later learn was called Bradley Creek. The road hung on the left shoulder above the creek bottom, in the shadow of a steep hillside marked by scattered piñon, cedar, and juniper. The creek was thick with willows, abandoned prospect holes showed higher up the shoulders, and the road bent to the east before turning back to the south, crossing the creek to begin to mount a bench to cross over the rolling foothills.

Eli reined up as they crested the bench, choosing to make a scan of the countryside to know where they were, what the land was like. Below them, the buff-colored hills rolled away, sometimes topping out with mesas or plateaus, but always showing sagebrush, greasewood, rabbitbrush, and lots of cacti. Near them, the beginning of the massive valley held clusters of tall cottonwoods, each cluster standing alone and adding its bouquet of green to the otherwise dull land. A long line of blue mountains shouldered up to the green of the valley with their pines that painted the hills a dark blue, marred only by rimrock of grey granite. In the far distance, higher mountains scratched at the blue of the sky with their pointed granite peaks, their necklines showing the timberline of black timber. Snow still showed in the ravines and gorges of the high country.

Eli looked back left at the long and wide blanket of green that carpeted the valley bottom. It was a fertile land where game was plentiful and beauty was abundant, only to be marred by the lust of men searching for the yellow metal that would make them rich. A few rough cabins, log walled and sod roofed, hung on the creek banks, overlooking rockers and sluice boxes, some already abandoned and left to decay in the hot sun.

Several creeks meandered lazily through the wide valley, all marked by thick willows and alders, cotton-wood groves, and a variety of berry bushes and more. Eli preferred high ground, but his only choice was to drop away from the road, moving a little east with the creeks and find a good site among the cottonwoods for their camp. He looked left to a flat-topped butte that stood about three hundred feet higher than the valley bottom and would offer him a good promontory for a look around before the sun tucked itself away beyond the far blue mountains.

# CHAPTER 3

## TROUBLES

Eli sat with his knees drawn up, his elbows on his knees as he scanned the flats by the pale morning light. He had climbed the flat-top butte, leaving the youngsters in camp, but he had told Christine where he was headed. After his short time of prayer and reading a chapter of Psalms in the Bible, he had taken to his promontory to get a better lay of the land. A creek that fell from the high mountains and meandered through the foothills had enticed a small herd of elk to take their morning water and graze the nearby grass. They were a little over a mile away and most of the cows were keeping their orange-shaded calves close by as the herd cow lifted her head, looking downstream and into the valley below. Eli swung his binoculars to see what had caught her attention and saw six riders come from a camp in the cottonwoods.

He focused his glasses on the men, watched as they approached the road of the Bozeman Trail and stopped. One man turned to face the others and was obviously giving them instructions about something. When he finished, the group split up by twos, moving out to the road and starting south. The pairs spaced out, leaving at least a mile between them, and moving at a good pace but not in a hurry. Eli also noticed they had no pack-horses, nothing on their mounts that showed any excess of supplies, but that could just mean they were bound for the nearest town and nothing more, but something about the group just did not feel right to Eli. Why space out? Why not travel together? Unless they were intent on something that they did not want anyone to suspect.

He finished his scan of the valley and started back to the camp. As he stepped through the trees, he was surprised to see Christine already busy at the little fire, the coffeepot dancing on the rock, and the youngsters already downing their breakfast. He smiled when he saw they had another serving of johnnycakes with honey but understood their desire for the sweetness. Christine looked up as he neared, reached for the coffeepot and poured him a cup as he leaned his rifle against the grey trunk of an old cottonwood, and seated himself facing the fire. As he accepted the cup, he grinned, "I didn't think you three would be outta your blankets yet."

Narcissa beamed, "We are always early risers! My Pa used to say, 'If we're not up with the sun, we're missing the best part of the day!'" As she realized what she had said, she dropped her eyes and glanced to her little brother, then reached her arm around his shoulders and said something softly to him and pulled him close. Eli knew it would be hard for them in the coming days as they realized the gravity of their loss, but right now it was just the unbearable hurt of not seeing their mother and father around the fire like had been their custom.

Christine sat back with her own plate on her lap,

bowed her head for a moment, then looked up at Eli, "Will we make it to Nevada City today?"

He nodded, "We should make it to Virginia City. Nevada City is further on, but if we still have daylight, we might make it to Nevada City."

"I hope so. We want to see our Uncle Liam and Aunt Eireann." She nodded to her siblings, "Jackson was but a wee lad when last we saw them. It was nigh unto three, four years ago."

"Well, if we're going to get very far, we best be gettin' a move on then," suggested Eli, standing and tossing the dregs of his coffee on the remaining coals of the morning's fire. The youngsters jumped to their feet and began cleaning things up, washing the pans and such in the little creek and putting them away in the panniers. It was but a short while before all was ready, and they were mounted up and taking to the road. As Eli led out, he was mindful of the six men he saw earlier and wondered again just what they might be up to, mischief of some sort, no doubt.

By late morning, with the Madison River in sight off to the left, the road rounded the point of a low bluff that marked the end of the higher mountains to the west. The road kept to the shoulder, then dipped down to cross a little creek that showed sign of high water from the spring runoff with debris high up on the sloping banks. The road rounded another low shoulder and turned to the west, pointing back toward the long line of rolling foothills. Eli guessed they had covered close to ten miles when, just before the road crossed the creek, he dropped off and took to the creek bottom, looking for some grass and fresh water for the horses and mule as well as to give the youngsters a break from riding.

When they took to the road again, the Bozeman Trail

hugged the south-facing slope above a small creek in the bottom, before doing a switchback to climb higher and point to the west again. As they topped out on a long bluff, a dust cloud showed before them and within moments, Eli heard the crack of a whip followed by the shouts and whistles of a jehu at the end of the lines of a stagecoach. He grinned and motioned to the others to clear the road as they moved aside to let the hard charging stagecoach pass. The driver and messenger waved as they passed, the driver or jehu loosening the lines to slow the six-up as they began to descend the long slope to the bottom. As they passed, Eli noticed the lettering over the door of the coach that had a full load inside and four more passengers up top. *Overland Mail and Express* shown in gold letters and Eli knew that was Ben Holladay's company that recently bought the line from A.J. Oliver and Company.

The sun was bright in their face when the road dipped into a coulee alongside Daylight Creek, but they dropped behind the sagebrush-covered ridge before the road turned back to the west to reveal Virginia City, cradled in a long basin between slow-rising foothills on either side. The valley was devoid of any trees, the only green showing was from the few remaining alders and willows along the banks of Daylight Creek as it pushed through the middle of town.

The two horses and a mule bearing their unusual riders rode through town, looking at the many storefronts, boardwalks, and variety of characters that ogled them who appeared to be as strange as they appeared to the residents. Eli did his best to appear nonchalant and disinterested as he took in the sights, trying to mentally mark anything and anyone that might be of help in his search for his sons. Most of the storefronts were taverns, but many were the variety of general stores and specialty stores that catered to the miners, their needs and their wants. He was surprised to see such an abundance of stores and taverns, but few hotels and eating houses. As they neared the end of the street, he saw two black-smiths but the sign on the last log building boldly stated it was a livery stable, just what they needed for the animals.

The last building they came to was the Smith and Boyd Livery Stable, doors wide open and one man with a leather apron that had seen many a soiled hand wiped on it, stood leaning against the door, one hand on his hip and the other holding the end of a smoking pipe in his teeth. A bound neckerchief held his hair at bay as he scowled at the three animals with four riders and what appeared to be heavy packs and nodded as Eli pulled up close, leaned on his pommel and asked, "Got room for two horses and a mule?"

"I do. Bring 'em on in, there's some empty stalls toward the rear an' a tack room at the back where you can store your goods." He frowned as he looked sidelong at the young'uns riding with one man, but he grinned at all the red hair and freckles. As they passed, "You young'uns look like you might be a bit o' Irish, that right?"

Christine frowned at the man, "What of it?!" and nudged the mule on past without looking back at the pipe smoker. Eli had already stepped down and was leading his horses to the back, looked to see if the girls were following on the mule and stopped at the empty stalls. He helped the girls down and began stripping the horses. "We'll leave the animals here and get us a room. Tomorrow we'll see 'bout gettin' you three some more clothes and such."

Christine came a little closer, nodded back toward the big doors, "I don't like that man back there. He asked if we were Irish, but he did it in a way I didn't like. It was as if he had something against our being Irish."

"Oh, I wouldn't worry about him. He might just be the friendly sort." He looked back to see the man approaching, and asked, "You the owner?"

"One of 'em. I recently partnered with the fella that started it. I think he's wanting to move on, maybe try looking for gold like all the rest of 'em." He puffed on his pipe as he leaned back against the gate of a stall, watching the youngsters help with the packs and panniers. When they finished stacking their gear in the tack room, Eli stood with his bedroll and saddlebags on one arm, his rifle cradled in the crook of the other, and asked, "Where's the nearest hotel?"

The man looked at Eli, glanced to the youngsters, "The Fairweather Inn is 'cross the street, down a ways. Not far." He nodded to the youngsters, "All them your'n?"

"For now," answered Eli. "So, you're one of the owners? Which one, Smith or Boyd?"

"I'm Smith, Liam Smith."

Eli frowned, glanced to see Christine wide-eyed as she looked from the liveryman to her brother and sister and back. She asked, "Did you say, Liam Smith?"

The liveryman nodded, puffed on his pipe, "That's right."

"Is your wife named Eireann?" asked Christine, almost breathless as she spoke.

The liveryman nodded, frowning, "How'd you guess that?"

"You have a sister named Katherine?"

"Aye," he slowly answered, frowning.

Christine rushed to the man and threw her arms around him, burying her face in his chest and the man, surprised, even shocked, looked askance to Eli who stood grinning. Eli explained, "That is Christine Doherty, and those two are Narcissa and Jackson. And if I'm right, they are your sister's children."

The man pushed Christine back to look at her, smiled broadly, "Aye, it is you! That's why I asked about your Irish." He looked about, "But, where's your tuisti, your Máthair and Athair?" Christine dropped her eyes, shaking her head and could not answer.

Eli spoke up, "Their wagon train was hit by a war party of Sioux, wiped 'em all out. The youngsters hid out in the brush at the creek," he paused, and motioned to the stalls, "had their mule with 'em, and I found 'em after. We were headed to Nevada City, that's where they said you and their pa was going to be partners or something."

"Yeah, but I was talkin' to Boyd, and he needed some help, so I bought in with him. Then everything slowed down and folks started leavin', goin' to Last Chance, and well, things change." He dropped to one knee and hugged the two younger children, stood to put an arm over Christine's shoulders, and grinned, "Your Aunt Eireann will be happy to see you three!" He looked back to Eli, "We'll want them with us, we've got extra room and the house next to ours is empty too. You're welcome to stay with us."

Eli grinned, "I'm gonna get me a room at the Inn, then I was going to take these three to dinner, and if there's any stores still open, they'll be needing some clothes and such." He pulled his pocket watch from his vest pocket, popped the lid open, and saw it was five thirty, "You closing up soon?"

He shook his head, "Don't usually shut down till dark an' that won't be for about two hours."

"Then we'll just drop my gear at the Inn, and we'll see 'bout gettin' them some more duds." He grinned, looked at the three, and asked, "You want to get something to eat or get some new clothes?"

Jackson spoke up, "Let's eat!" and hid behind Narcissa.

"Alright then, let's eat!" declared Eli, with a nod to Liam. As the kids headed for the door, Eli said, "If we're not back before you close up shop, you'll know where we'll be."

Liam grinned, nodding, and said to the kids, "Don't eat too much, you won't fit in your new clothes!" and chuckled as he waved them out the door.

# CHAPTER 4

## INQUIRIES

The rising sun showed distant mountains as silhouettes of jagged teeth, but nearer to town, the flattop buttes drew a long line of shadows across the eastern horizon. Eli walked into the sun, ducking under a few overhangs of porches as his boots clattered on the boardwalk. A lop-eared lazy dog slapped his tail against the boardwalk and lifted one eye to the early riser as he walked past. Eli grinned, thinking that every Western town seemed to have one of those dogs that were lazy beggars and did little to earn their spot on the boardwalk. He walked past the *Montana Post* newspaper office, the door standing open and a man sitting at a desk, garters holding his sleeves up as he labored over the day's headlines. He paid no attention as Eli walked past, nodded, and kept going. At the next corner, Eli crossed to the south side of the main road through the middle of town, and started back to the west, the sun warming his back.

He had spotted three places he wanted to look into, two mercantile stores, a café, and the sheriff's office. But first things first, he thought he heard a cup of hot coffee calling his name and he turned into the café that was sandwiched between the two mercantile stores. He dropped into a chair at a table by the window, faced the door and watched as a man with a drooping moustache, spotted apron, and sleepy eyes, nodded as he leaned on the counter, looking at the newcomer. "What can I get'cha?" he called to Eli.

"Coffee, and whatever you have ready for breakfast."

The man nodded, straightened up, and turned back to go through the doorway to the kitchen. He soon returned with a tin cup and a coffeepot, poured the cup full, and asked, "Eggs'n taters alright?"

"That'll do fine," Eli answered, as the man turned away not waiting for a reply. Eli grinned, shook his head, and picked up a newspaper that lay on the bay windowsill. The *Montana Post* of July 7th, 1866. He saw the announcement of the Great Beaverhead Wagon Road that was now open and that it went through Beaverhead Valley and Stinkingwater, with a cutoff to Helena, Confederate and Blackfoot country.

There was also an announcement that the Planter's House Hotel was renovated and open for business. News told of Ward's rolling mill being burned causing a loss of $200,000. He had just started to glance over several columns regarding political movements in Washington but was pleasantly interrupted by the delivery of a plate of eggs and potatoes and a refill on his coffee. He nodded his thanks to the cook/waiter, bowed his head for a quick prayer of thanks, but when he looked up, was surprised to see the man sit down opposite him and pour himself a cup of coffee as he joined Eli.

The man grinned up at Eli as he finished pouring his coffee, "You're new, ain't'cha?"

Eli grinned, nodded, and answered, "If you mean am I new to Virginia City, then yes I am, but otherwise I'm too old to be new at much of anything else."

The cook chuckled, "I'm Micah, but most folks just call me Cooky. Been here goin' on four years now, seen most of 'em come'n go. Now they be goin' to Last Chance Gulch, but there's some still hangin' on. You lookin' fer gold like the rest of 'em?"

Eli had a mouthful and had to finish chewing, wash it down with some coffee, before he answered. "No, I'm not after gold, but I am lookin' for something." He reached into his pocket and brought out the tintype of his stepsons, "They are Joshua and Jubal Paine, my stepsons. I'm looking for them. Last word I had on them was they were coming this way, and they are looking for gold."

Micah picked up the tintype, looked at the picture of the twins, and looked at Eli, "They must favor their ma."

Eli chuckled, "Yup," he grinned as he nodded, "She's the one that sent me after 'em. I promised I'd try to get 'em to go back home, but I have to find them first."

"I don't recall seein' them, twins'd be hard to miss, less'n they was separated. But, they don't look familiar to me." He took a long sip of his coffee, "An' if'n they was lookin' fer gold, they might be a little hard-pressed what with that Californy bunch movin' in."

Eli frowned, "What's that about?"

"Oh, you know some folks. They think they know more'n others an' they got the answer to ever'thin'. From what I hear, this bunch has some new way o' minin' they call hydraulic minin'. It's where they have high-powered water what washes the whole crick bank down an' into the sluice boxes, can wash away a whole hillside in one day!"

Eli frowned, although he had heard about hydraulic mining, they would still have to have the claims on the land before they could use that method. He looked at Cooky, "But if the others have their claims, what then?"

Cooky chuckled, "That's just it. There's a few claims that have been abandoned, but most have been bought out by their neighbors an' such, but these fellers are comin' in an' buyin' or just takin' over the claims, mostly just takin' 'em over, runnin' the other miners off. But, it's just what I heerd, mind you. I ain't *seen* nuthin'."

"What about the law?"

"Onliest law we got is miners law, an' most o' the miners pulled out fer Last Chance. Them what's left ain't enough to do much, an' the sheriff, wal, he just tends to things in the towns, lets the miners handle their own problems."

"Isn't that what led to the vigilantes?"

"Ummhmm, but even the leaders of the vigilantes pulled out after the sheriffs were appointed an' the judges came in since this hyar is now the territory capitol."

"I think I met one of the leaders of the vigilantes, John Beidler."

Micah grinned, nodding, as he sipped his coffee. "That's him alright. Whar'dja run into him?"

"Helena. He helped handle some river pirates."

"Hang 'em, did he?"

Eli nodded, finishing his breakfast. Micah stood, topped off Eli's coffee and with a nod, went back to the kitchen. Several others had come in and a woman had put on an apron and was taking orders as Eli picked up the paper and read a bit more. On page two he read about the debate between the Democrats and Republicans regarding the disposition of the southern states.

The Democrats wanted Negro suffrage to be ordained, while the Republicans were fighting for the rights of the Negroes. While the southern Democrat states wanted to represent the Negroes, but deny them all political rights, the Republicans wanted to restrict the representatives to represent the number of voters instead of the population that included the Negroes, unless and until the Negroes had the same rights as declared under the new laws.

Eli shook his head and lay the paper back in the windowsill, thinking all the while about having fought a war and watched thousands die while the politicians were still arguing many of the same things that brought about the war. He rose from his seat, doing his best to not let the tidbits in the paper ruin his good breakfast. He pushed the door open and stepped onto the board-walk. He saw a man walk into the sheriff's office and decided to go see the man before buying more supplies.

The sign in the window said *Andrew J. Snyder, Sheriff, Madison County, Montana Territory*. Eli walked into the open door, nodded to the man seated at the desk, and extended his hand, "Sheriff, I'm Eli McCain."

The sheriff stood and extended his hand to shake, motioned to the chair. Both were seated as the sheriff answered, "And I'm Sheriff Snyder, how can I help you, young man?"

Eli looked up at the man with a high brow and widow's peaks that pointed to the thick hair that showed white. His hair was down to his collar, combed back and down almost like a woman's and showing the vanity of the man who ran his fingers through the thick hair above his ears and leaned back in the chair. He was a big man, his potbelly pushing aside the leather vest to show itself and the tight linen shirt that strained at the buttons. The sheriff interlocked his fingers as his hands rested on the paunch, and grinned at the visitor.

Eli thought the man to be no older than he was, despite the white at the temples and through his dark straight hair. His face and hands showed no wrinkles and Eli guessed him to be the type that thought of himself as a father figure to the people of his town and any others that might visit, no matter their age. If he could establish that relationship, then keeping everyone in check would be a little easier if they thought of him like another father figure.

But Eli slowly shook his head as he fought back a grin, "Well, Sheriff, I was plannin' on pokin' around your territory, asking questions, and I thought it best to let you know what I was here about." He dug out the tintype and pushed it across the desk, "Those are my boys, twins Jubal and Joshua. They left home before their mother died, and she made me promise to find them and try to get them to go back home." He accepted the picture back from the sheriff and continued, "They were seen up by Montana City, and the woman that grub-staked them said they were prospecting in the mountains for the mother lode," he chuckled when he said that as did the sheriff, "but they did get a little, and she thought they might head to Confederate Gulch."

The sheriff leaned forward, elbows on the desk, "Wal stranger, you're in the wrong place for Confederate Gulch, that's up by—" He was stopped when Eli held up a hand as he nodded.

"I know, I know, but they were seen at Jefferson City after that and were said to be coming to Virginia City. So..." explained Eli, leaning back in his chair. "I thought I best check with you, see if they had gotten into any trouble or such-like, then I plan to work my way toward Nevada City and beyond, see what I find."

"Well, I don't know about your boys, but if you go pokin' around and askin' questions, you might get yourself in trouble. There's been some other newcomers that have been pokin' around, and some report they've run off the claim owners, bought others out, and seem to be takin' over." He shook his head and leaned back, "There's only one of me, and from what I hear, there's maybe six or more of them. And they got the backin' of some big outfit outta California that's wantin' to bring in hydraulic mining. Now, they ain't been doin' nothin' close to Virginia City, most of what I hear is just reports from some disgruntled, down on their luck miners, and I don't know what to make of it. 'Sides, like I said, there's only one of me an' I can't cover the whole shebang by my lonesome."

Eli frowned, looked at the tired man sitting behind the desk, "I might have seen those men between here and Jefferson City. The one that looked like the leader was ridin' a mighty fancy horse, a blaze-faced sorrel with waxen mane and tail, three stockings."

"Yup, that's them. But..." he shrugged and held his open hands out to his sides.

# CHAPTER 5

## ISSUES

The town was coming alive as Eli left the sheriff's office. Wagons from the nearby farms and mines were rolling in, most driven by one man, some with an additional man and a pair carried a man and a woman. Those with couples were obviously from the farms hereabout while the others were lone men, too tired to wash up and concerned only about their needs. Apart from the sheriff, Eli knew the best place to get any news would be the taverns and cafés. He had already garnered most of the local gossip from Micah at the Miner's Café, so he thought he would try a few of the taverns, after that maybe the general stores where he could buy his supplies.

Just around the corner from the café and the sheriff's office, the Pony Saloon showed four horses standing hipshot at the hitchrail. Eli shook his head and pushed through the doors. He stepped to the side, letting his eyes adjust to the dim light, and took a few long strides to come to the bar where a tall skinny barkeep with too much hair was wiping down the bar top. Three men sat at a corner table, one man, a bit larger than the others, appeared to be holding court as the two men leaned into the conversation. Two others stood at the far end of the bar, talking to one another as they cornered the counter. The barkeep looked to Eli, stopped his wiping the counter, and flipped the rag over his shoulder as he asked, "What'll it be?"

"I see you've got some coffee on that stove over yonder. How 'bout some of that?"

"This ain't no café!" grumbled the barkeep as he started for the stove.

"No, but it's a mite early for me to start drinkin' anything else," answered Eli, watching the man walk away.

The two at the end of the bar heard the repartee and turned to face Eli. The bigger of the two, who sported about a week's worth of whiskers and the same amount of dirt, snarled, "If you was a real man, ain't never too early to be drinkin' a man's drink!"

Eli ignored the man and his attempt at arousing the ire of a stranger to the town. Eli knew there was at least one in every town and every saloon, a wannabe bad man that tried to climb his way to power by stepping on anyone that he thought might be a good stepping stone, anyone he could bully or harangue to make himself appear to be a big man that others should fight shy of, at least in his own mind. When Eli refused to take the bait, the ruffian turned to face him and spoke even louder, "Whatsamatta you, you deef as you are stupid? I said, you ain't a real man if'n you cain't drink anytime o' the day!"

Eli slowly turned to face the man, his elbows on the bar as he accepted the steaming cup of coffee from the barkeep, who whispered to him as he sat the cup down,

"Watch yourself. That's Frank Kelso an' he's always lookin' for a fight, guns or fists. He's a bad'un." Eli gave a slight nod and still refused to take the bait of the bully and lifted his cup for a sip of the hot brew.

The big-mouth bully strode down the bar to side Eli, slammed his fist on the bar, and growled, "I'm talkin' to you! Pay 'tention!"

Eli sat his cup down, turned just his head to look at the man who stood just over six feet tall, broad shoulders and chest, but his belly hung over his belt about as far as his attitude. He started to grab Eli's shoulder, but the cocking of the hammer on Eli's Colt stopped him. Eli had slipped the Colt from the holster as he lifted the coffee cup, knowing that most would think a butt forward meant it had to be drawn with his right hand, but Eli was more than capable with either hand. Kelso looked down to see the one-eyed barrel that was cradled in the crook of Eli's elbow and pointed dead center at his chest. Eli spoke softly, "Were you talkin' to me?" as he turned his head slightly to scowl at the man.

The big man slowly lifted both hands, palms forward, eyes wide as he stammered and started backpedaling, "Uh, no, no. I was just funnin', din't mean nuttin'! Sorry mister!"

Eli nodded and looked to the shocked barkeep who had stepped back away from the bar, one hand on the bar rag, the other against the counter behind him. He was as startled as the bully and looked wide-eyed at Eli, then to the bully as he backed away to join his partner at the end of the bar. He looked back to Eli, and said, "Mister, you just made my day! I don't know how many times I've seen him try to pick a fight or even start one and always come out on top. That's the first time I've seen him take water." He looked down at Eli's cup, "Let me get you a refill!"

When the barkeep returned, Eli took out his tintype and explained about his search for his boys. When the barkeep had no news, Eli said if he saw them or heard about twins working together, to leave word with the sheriff. As they talked, Eli looked in the mirror and watched the two men walk past to exit the saloon. When he finished his conversation and coffee, he asked the barkeep, "Those two, are they back shooters? Think they might be waitin' for me?"

"Mister, I wouldn't trust them if they were locked in a cell and had shackles on. Even then, I wouldn't turn my back on 'em. They've been rumored to do just about anything. Never worked an honest day in their life, but always have money or gold dust."

Eli expressed his thanks and turned to leave as the man called out, "Watch yourself, Kelso ain't about to forget what happened." Eli waved over his shoulder as he pushed through the doors and stepped onto the board-walk. Always watchful, he stepped into the shadows and looked the street over. The saloon was around the corner from the main street, which was called Wallace, but he saw nothing alarming and stepped out on the boardwalk and headed west toward the livery. He remembered two places, The Buford Store and McClurg and Ptorney Mercantile, where he would get his supplies, and a saloon next to the livery, Stoer Saloon.

The Buford Store had the foodstuffs that Eli needed and after filling the order, Eli showed the tintype and asked about the boys, but they were unknown. He went to the mercantile and bought additional ammunition for his weapons and got the same response to his inquiry. As he walked past the saloon, he saw a couple of horses that looked to be the same as had been hitched at the Pony Saloon, the obvious one being a strawberry roan that was not a common color. He went to the livery, stashed his supplies with his gear, and returned to the saloon.

As he thought, the two ruffians were in the saloon, but this time were seated at a table in a dark corner with two other men. As he started to the bar, he saw the two tell the others about him as they all turned to look, but Eli acted as if he had not seen them, moving straight to the bar. When the bartender came near, Eli asked for a beer and was served a big mug of foaming beer. As it was set before him, he brought out the tintype and asked the usual question of the bartender, but before the man could answer, he looked past Eli, eyes wide, and leaned back away from the bar.

Eli saw the movement of Kelso as he came up on Eli's right, but the sound of a cocking hammer came from his left and slightly behind him. The voice behind him said, "Put that Colt on the bar!" As Eli slowly complied, Kelso stepped to the bar beside him.

Kelso slid down the bar, came close, and growled, "Now we'll see just what kinda man you are!" as he grabbed at Eli's shoulder to pull him around. As Eli was turned, Kelso cocked back his right fist, but Eli buried his left deep in Kelso's gut, bending him over as he gasped for air, but his face met Eli's right uppercut that splattered his nose across his face, splashing blood on the bar and the man's front. Eli was no stranger to bare-knuckle fighting, having spent some time with John Morrissey, the Irish born, California and New York raised, bare-knuckle champion that had defeated Yankee Sullivan to take the crown.

Kelso staggered back, stumbling over a spittoon and fell. His arms flung out as he fought to catch himself. Eli turned to face the man behind him who held his pistol limply, shocked at the sudden attack by Eli as he watched his friend fall back.

Eli threw a left jab to the man's face, a roundhouse right to his jaw and heard the crack of bone as the man dropped his pistol, grabbing at Eli, but caught only air as his head was snapped to the side. Eli stepped in and delivered a storm of blows to the man's middle, driving him back toward the door. Eli stepped back, watched the man grabbing at the chairs as he crashed over the table, all the while trying to draw breath through a bloodied mouth.

The clatter of chairs turned Eli to catch a massive fist aimed at his face, but he turned away just enough to make it a glancing blow. He countered with a flurry of fists to Kelso's big gut, each time burying the fists deep, robbing Kelso of the ability to catch his wind and as he bent over, he was again met with the uppercut of Eli that smashed Kelso's lips against broken teeth, and another that broke his jaw. Eli stepped back, looked at the two that still sat at the table. Kelso's partner began to rise to his feet, dragging iron as he did, but Eli snatched the LeMat from his back and cocked the hammer as he brought it around, "Don't do it! Drop that pistol!" ordered Eli. The barked order, like so many others he had given in the war, demanded obedience and the man showed a pale face, mouth hanging open, as he dropped his pistol to the sawdust floor.

Eli looked at the seated man, who held both hands high, and answered, "I ain't a part of this!"

"Then clear out!" ordered Eli, moving back to the bar so he could keep the three in sight. He watched the fourth man leave and motioned to Kelso's partner, "Drag your friends outta here!" he barked, breathing heavy but in total control. He watched as the three, leaning on one another, staggered from the saloon, then stuffed the LeMat in his belt at his back, picked up his Colt and holstered it, and leaned on the bar to catch his breath.

The bartender looked at Eli, "Mister, I don't know who you are, but you just did what I've been wantin' to see for a long time. That bunch is trouble wherever they go, and now they've joined up with that gang from California and are playing hob with the miners. But I'm thinkin' you shoulda gone on and killed 'em, cuz they won't be forgettin' this, you can sure bet on it. But you sure notched their branch, yessir!"

"Maybe so, but I had enough killin' in the war. The way I see it, any man can make a mistake and learn from it, but there's no learning when they're dead," mulled Eli, turning toward the door to leave. As he stepped from the saloon, he remembered his time with Morrissey when they both were courting the daughter of a ship's captain employed by Eli's shipbuilding family out of their company on the Essex River. He had introduced Morrissey to the girl and the man that would later be known as Old Smoke, won her heart and her hand. Eli chuckled at the thought, relieved that he had dodged the bullet all too soon in his young military life and remained single for a while longer. He glanced heavenward, remembering his wife, who had been the wife of his good friend and West Point classmate, Lieutenant Ferdinand Paine, who asked Eli to take care of her as he lay dying after a skirmish where he took a bullet. Eli had married her, pregnant with twins, and gave her his name and honor, and spent as much time as possible with her during his military career, only to come home to her on her dying bed.

# CHAPTER 6

## DAYLIGHT

Liam and Eireann Smith, the uncle and aunt of the youngsters brought in by Eli, had their home behind the livery and overlooking the drop-off to the cattail-filled bog at creek bottom. They had invited Eli to join them for supper and Eli wanted the opportunity to see the kids again and tell them goodbye before he started out toward Nevada City and points northwest in his search for the twins. Liam was sitting in a rocking chair on their porch when Eli stepped through the gate of the fence around their front yard. "Welcome, Eli!" greeted Liam, leaning forward and waving. "C'mon up and grab a seat, supper'll be ready right soon."

Eli responded, "Liam," with a nod as he started up the three steps to the porch. A long bench sat before the windows and stretched across most of the porch and a wave of the hand from Liam directed Eli to have a seat. The door opened and Eireann stepped out, holding a steaming cup of coffee, "I heard Liam greet you and thought you might like to have a cup of coffee." She smiled as she handed the cup to a standing Eli, and added, "I'm Eireann, Liam's wife, and it's welcome you are to our home."

"I'm pleased to meet you, ma'am; the youngsters spoke of you both."

"Please, sit," she answered, nodding to the bench. "And they have not stopped talking about you either." She dropped her eyes, moved a step closer to her man, and added, "We are so grateful to you for bringing them to us. And they said you buried the people of the wagon train, so, we're thankful for that as well."

"There was little else I could do, there were so many. In this country, it's not a good thing to mark graves as there are those that would dig them up and mutilate the bodies, so, they were buried together, unmarked. I'm sorry."

"Oh, there's nothing for you to be sorry about, you did more than most would. The children's father was my brother, and their mother was Liam's sister. And for you to take on the children...we are so very thankful," explained Eireann. "Please, enjoy your coffee, the supper will be ready right soon." She turned away and disappeared into the house.

The men sat silently for a moment, savoring the coffee, until Liam looked to Eli, "And what will you do now, Eli?"

"I've been on a search for my boys, twins, that ran off from home and their mother made me promise before she died, that I would try to find them and get them to go back home. The last word I had on them was that they were coming to Alder Gulch and try their luck."

"They know anything about gold mining?" asked Liam.

Eli chuckled, "'Bout the same as most of these gold blinded men, not much."

Liam nodded, shaking his head, "Ain't that the truth. I've run into a bunch of 'em, and if you was to add up all the things that the whole bunch knows, it wouldn't be enough to fill a brass spittoon. And the spittoon would already hold more worth than what most of 'em find." He paused, chuckling, "Oh, there's some of 'em that find color, but they spend it faster'n they make it. Then they hear about 'nother strike some'eres else and off they go, chasin' the dream!"

"Supper's ready," called Eireann. "How 'bout you fellas comin' in and let's get started?"

When they entered the home, the table was spread with several filled dishes and the house held many delightful aromas of hot food. Narcissa and Jackson were standing behind the chairs on one side, Eireann and Christine were on the other, and the chairs at either end stood empty, waiting for the men. Eli took the chair at the end beside Christine and Jackson, stood behind the chair and waited for Liam. As he took his place, Liam said, "Let us give thanks," and bowed his head. He began with thanks for food and family, for bringing the children to their home, for the guardian angel named Eli, and for the many blessings they had been given. He finished with an "Amen," that was echoed by everyone at the table.

The children were continually chattering about their new home, family, and the possibility of going to school. They were excited to share all the new things with the man that had been their only friend and protector for several days, the worst days of their young lives, but he had given them a special friendship that helped them and delivered them. Now that they had a new home, family, and future, they were excited once again. Christine was the more morose of the trio, but she did her best to be a part of the excitement. When the meal was over and it was time to go, he spent a moment with each one, promised he would return and gave each one a warm hug. Christine held on for a moment, then looked up at Eli, "Thank you, Eli. We would not have survived without you."

Eli chuckled, "Oh, I don't know about that. You and the youngsters are tougher'n you think. But you don't have to worry about that now, your Aunt Eireann and Uncle Liam will take fine care of you." A brief embrace and he turned away to leave.

Liam waited on the porch and walked with Eli down to the gate, "I know you're going north along Daylight Creek, but I've heard some things that say you need to be mighty careful. There's a gang of men that're trying to take over everything, and if your boys are workin' on the Daylight, they might run into trouble, and you, too, for that matter."

"I've heard about them, the troublemakers I mean, but I need to find my boys, so..." He shrugged as he pushed open the gate. He stood for a moment, looked back at Liam, "You've got your hands full with those three. They're good kids, all of 'em, and they'll be a blessing to you. But, they'll also give you a lot of headaches and probably a few heartaches, but that's young'uns for you. Be sure to hug 'em for me ever' now and then and tell 'em I'll be back to check on 'em."

"You do that, and welcome. But you be careful, like I said, and don't trust anyone!" replied Liam, as he stepped away from the gate to return to the porch.

———

THE SUN HAD YET to crest the long flat-top mesa that rose above Virginia City and before it showed its face, Eli was riding into Nevada City. With less than two miles behind him, he spotted a café with a sign that simply read, *Ma's Café*. He reined up, nudged Rusty, his long-legged claybank stallion to the hitchrail, slapped the reins around the rail, and did the same with the lead rope of the grey packhorse. He stepped up on the board-walk and pushed into the café, found a table, and sat down. His eyes were adjusting to the light when a woman stood between him and the window, hands on hips, as she asked, "Well?"

"Coffee and whatever you have for a breakfast, please."

"Humph," she mumbled as she moved away, "Men!" she added, just loud enough for Eli to hear. When she returned, the sun shone on her and Eli could see she was a hefty woman with a crooked nose, a scowl for a face, but Eli saw a touch of mischief in her eyes. As she poured his coffee, Eli said, "Thank you, ma'am."

"Ain't no ma'am, I'se a miss, but most just call me Ma."

"Pleased to meet'chu, Ma. I'm Eli."

"Humph," she grunted, and turned away. Eli grinned, turned his attention to his coffee, and lifted the cup of hot brew to his lips as he looked out the window. When Ma returned, she had the coffeepot in one hand and a big plate of steaming food in the other. She sat the plate in front of Eli, poured the cup full, and started to turn away, when Eli asked, "Ma, could I ask you something?"

She frowned, turned around and Eli handed her the tintype of the boys. "Those are my stepsons; I've been looking for them for a while and last word was they were headed thisaway."

Ma sat the coffeepot down, picked up the tintype, and turned so the sunlight would shine on the picture. She looked at the boys, looked at Eli, and back to the boys. "You can sure tell they ain't yourn. Must favor their ma, good thing too. You ain't much to look at." She chuckled, let a slow smile split her face, and handed the tintype back to Eli. "Ain't seen 'em. You gonna be aroun' a while, lookin' fer 'em?"

"I will. I plan on working my way downstream, check with the miners and anyone else I see, and if I don't find them, well…" he shrugged and pulled the plate close. "If you see 'em, could you pass word to Sheriff Snyder over at Virginia City?"

"If'n I see 'em," she declared, as she picked up the pot and went to the kitchen.

Eli enjoyed his breakfast of eggs, bacon, fried pota-toes, and biscuits with honey. He sat back, sipping on his refilled cup of coffee and looked out the window at some riders passing by and what he saw caused him to sit up when a big sorrel with flaxen mane and tail passed and riding beside that man was a familiar face on a straw-berry roan. There were seven men, riding two by two as if in a cavalry formation, but they were not as neat as military, most unshaven and scruffy-looking, as they scowled at anyone that looked their way. Eli shook his head, *That's trouble for sure!*

# CHAPTER 7

# BEAR GULCH

"Are you sure about this?" asked Jubal, looking at his brother as they rode the Mullan Road to the west.

"Like I told you before, Jubal, why have we been listening to what others have to say, like the two in Prickly Pear Gulch, or those two in the bar at the Red Rooster, or even Madame Beauchamp? If they know so much and are so certain about the strikes and claims that they talked about, why aren't they packin' up and headin' out to get all that easy gold? I'm tellin' you, this article right here," he waved the folded-up newspaper before him, "says it right. It's written from reports that came in from the actual strikes, and it's the newest gold find. We can get there before the real crowds do and maybe get a better chance at a real claim!"

"But we ain't the only ones that can read a newspaper, and what was that you said, 'almost a hundred cabins already'?" grumbled Jubal.

Joshua shook his head, "But what you're missing is where it says there are claims that are held at ten thousand dollars and others are saying the area is 'extremely rich'! It also says the 'pay dirt is six to eight feet deep,' that ain't much! He said the Bear Gulch, Elk Gulch, Deep Gulch, and more are showing color and that each pan pays twelve to fifty cents—per pan!"

They rode in silence for a while, each one thinking about the possibilities. How much work it would be to dig six to eight feet deep to get paydirt, and how many pans would it take to make a good day of wages? The brothers soon were showing smiles on their faces at the thoughts that stirred their spirits. Joshua broke the silence, "Something else I been thinkin'. Have you noticed how many men work their fingers to the bone, digging and grubbing in the dirt, and get discouraged and leave? Seems to be a lot more that barely make eatin' money and not even that, and they either just give up and leave, or turn bad. What we both kinda missed, the very last part of this article says, 'Flour is $36 per sack; bacon, ninety cents per pound; beans, forty cents, and all other provisions in proportion.'"

He tucked the folded-up paper back into his saddle-bags and leaned on the pommel as the horses steadily trudged down the trail, "Seems to me the only ones really makin' money are the merchants and such that are chargin' those prices. You know, like the freighters we worked for out of Fort Benton."

"Yeah, I think you're right about that. But still, a big strike…" mulled Jubal, visions of riches dancing in his mind.

"But for every one that makes a big strike, there's at least a dozen merchants standing in line with their hands out to get their share, and they get a share of every strike, not just one."

The little creek that sided the Mullan Road fed into

the Little Blackfoot River and the road turned westward. Where they came through the foothills, the rolling terrain was dimpled with juniper, but now the hills to the south were black with thick timber—fir, spruce, and pines crowded each other for soil and sun, while the lazy river twisted its way through the long and wide valley that showed an abundance of green. The Mullan Road kept to the shoulders of the hills and buttes that showed a few talus slopes but were mostly showing spreads of bunchgrass, gramma, sage, and more. Cottonwoods, alders, and willows crowded the banks of the Little Blackfoot River as the clear waters from high-country snowshed chuckled over gravelly shoals.

It had been a long day and as the Mullan Road made a bend to the south to cut through the rocky foothills that shouldered into the now narrow valley, Jubal spotted a likely campsite on the north side of the river where the cottonwoods pushed against the hills and offered good cover, out of sight of the road and any other travelers. With a wave of his hand, he led the way across the shallow waters, through the thickets of willow, and onto a small grassy flat that was hidden from sight.

They stripped and rubbed down their horses and the pack mule and while Jubal picketed the animals, Joshua began gathering wood for a fire. They shared the camp duties and soon had a small hat-sized fire under the wide-reaching branches of a thick cottonwood and with cornmeal biscuits baking in the dutch oven, the coffeepot dancing and giving off the smell of fresh brewed coffee, Joshua flipped the strip steaks from the deer they took that morning. Jubal was reaching for the coffeepot when a voice came from the trees, "Hello the camp! Can we come in, we're friendly."

Jubal snatched up his Henry, tossed the other one to

Joshua and they each jacked a round into the chamber and stood apart, as Jubal answered, "Come in, but keep your hands in sight and empty!"

Two men stepped through the thickets, leading their horses and hands held out, empty. Joshua and Jubal were surprised to see the men were Natives, but dressed like white men, hair short, hats and all. One stepped forward, grinning, "Ain't you never seen a white Indian?" he chuckled.

"Uh, no, can't say as I have. You're certainly not what we expected to see."

"We been surprising you white men for a long time." He chuckled and glanced from Jubal to Joshua, "Can we put our hands down?"

"Sure, but keep 'em away from them hoglegs you got strapped on your hip. I have a tendency to get *real* nervous and start pullin' on this trigger *real* easy."

The man grinned, "I'm Two Moons and this is Black Eagle, we're *Numunuu* or what you call Comanche." He looked at Joshua and to Jubal waiting, held out one hand, palm up, and shrugged.

Jubal grinned, "Oh, yeah. I'm Jubal and this is my brother, Joshua."

"Howdy, fellas," stated Two Moons with a glance to his partner.

Black Eagle nodded, looked at the coffeepot, "Got 'nuff to share?"

Joshua lowered his rifle, "Yeah. Got your own cups?"

The visitors nodded, turned to their saddlebags and retrieved the cups, and stepped closer to the fire and held them out. Joshua poured their cups full, glanced to Jubal and receiving a nod, he looked back to Two Moons, "We've got biscuits cookin', got some fresh venison if'n you wanna hang some strips over the fire?"

Without lowering his coffee cup, Two Moons nodded and sat down on the rocks nearby. He looked up at Jubal who still stood with his rifle at his side, "That's good java. Ain't had that good'a stuff since we left the trail drive?"

"Trail drive?" asked Jubal.

"Yeah. We were scoutin' for Nelson Story, he's bringing up a herd from Texas. We got 'em through the territory, an' after hearin' all the talk of the goldfields, we asked to leave so we could come ahead and have a look. That's where we're headin', heard about a strike up some place called Bear Gulch."

Black Eagle chimed in, nodding toward Two Moons, "He's lookin', me, I'm just along to see the country, maybe find something that pays reg'lar and ain't as dirty as herdin' cows!"

While the others talked, Joshua had sliced several thin strips of venison, fashioned a spit with green willows and hung the meat above the fire where it could catch the smoke and heat without the flames. He sat back and with a cup of coffee in hand, he looked at the two, and asked, "I ain't seen too many Natives dressed like cowboys and talking like white men. How'd that come to be?" He looked at the two, both with wide-brimmed hats, linen shirts, leather vests, denim britches with shotgun chaps, and Mexican-style boots and spurs, grinned a mite and looked at the two for an answer.

Two Moons chuckled, shaking his head slightly, "You ain't the first to ask that. We were raised by an old cattle rancher. He said we were the only survivors of a smallpox plague that struck the village of the Numunuu. Well, us and a woman. He took us all in, fed us, raised us, educated us, and took the woman as his wife. We were family and knew nothing else. Oh, we had a few memories of our village and people, we were eight and ten when he took us in, but mostly all we knew was what he taught us. He made us to be like the Mexican Vaqueros he hired, learned about cattle and ranchin' and such. But," he paused and looked at the ground and slowly shook his head, "He crossed over 'bout a year ago and the white man's law would not let us take over the ranch. So, White Feather, she was the woman he took in and was the only mother we knew, she went back to the people, the Comanche, and we knocked around a mite, took a few jobs as drovers, and when Story came along and needed scouts, well..." he shrugged.

Black Eagle added, "We dress like white men, talk like white men, work like white men, but still," he shook his head, gritting his teeth. "That's why Two Moons thinks we should try the goldfields, maybe get rich and go back south, get a ranch and..." he shrugged.

There was a short spell of awkward silence, until Jubal began, "We left home to join the army during the war, but soon learned we didn't take to soldierin', so we took off, came west and have been, well, searching. Kinda like you. We've done some freighting, worked for a couple men that had a good gold claim, did some prospectin' ourselves, and now, we're headin' to Bear Gulch, too."

Joshua leaned forward to check the steaks in the frying pan with the potatoes and onions, pulled the pan away from the flames and checked the strips on the spit. He looked at the visitors, "We've only got two plates."

"We don't have any plates, but as soon as those are ready, we will be too." Two Moons looked around, grinned, and slipped a big Bowie knife from a scabbard at his hip and went to a downed cottonwood tree trunk and using the knife and a rock, he split off two slabs of wood and returned, holding them out, "Now we've got plates!"

————

THE MEAL WAS QUICKLY DOWNED, the coffee drunk, and the men agreed to share the campsite for the night. When all four had stretched out, Jubal and Joshua on one side of the fire and the two visitors on the other, they soon drifted off to sleep, trusting the animals to warn of any problems. Jubal and Joshua had that unspoken communication often found with twin siblings and they had slept with their boots on and pistols under their saddles that cradled their heads.

It was not the most restful night, but it passed without incident and Two Moons was the first up, stirring up the coals and readying the fire for some more coffee. Jubal chuckled as he dug the Arbuckles out of the pannier and saw Two Moons standing, with the pot full of fresh water and holding it out for the coffee. By the time the coffee was ready, the others had rousted out and they began making plans to travel to Bear Gulch together.

# CHAPTER 8

## CLAIM JUMPERS

The Chinese were diligent workers, more concerned about the small details of a job than most. When the new discovery of gold in the Last Chance Gulch prompted many of the claim owners on Alder Gulch to abandon or sell their claims, many of the claims were taken over by Chinese, who were willing to do the extra work to get the last bit of gold from the placers. As Eli started from Nevada City, he saw several claims being worked by groups of Chinese, all of whom were friendly enough to the passerby.

He had gone less than two miles from Nevada City when he encountered the remains of a claim, recent destruction showed with a long-tom sluice broken up and scattered about, the long flume axed to pieces, the remains of a miner's tent lay in ashes, and the bodies of the two presumed claim owners had been dragged to the side beside a stake with a handwritten sign that stated, *This claim belongs to the Seinfeld Mining Co., No Trespassing!* He stood in his stirrups looking up and down the stream. With each claim being about two hundred feet square, the next claim upstream was that being worked by the Chinese, three stood at the edge of their claim, watching Eli. He looked downstream, saw no activity, and continued on, although with a passing thought of burying the two miners.

As he approached the next claim, it was evident it had been thoroughly worked and apparently abandoned, although there was a portion of a flume still standing, it had long ago begun to crumble in disrepair and weathering. Another stake bore a similar sign declaring ownership of this claim just like the adjoining claim with the dead bodies. Eli turned back to the previous claim and went to the two bodies, stepped down, and retrieved a shovel from his packs and gave a cursory examination of the dead men, both having been severely beaten and shot in the back of the head. Eli shook his head, knowing this was not a friendly sale, but a hostile takeover, and he had a good idea who it might have been.

The condition of the bodies told Eli the beatings had happened no earlier than the night before, perhaps even early on this same day. He began digging near the bodies, stacking rocks to the side, and shoveling the dirt to the other side. About a quarter hour passed and he paused, getting a breather. He watched as the three Chinese came near, shovels in hand, and began digging the second grave, one man spelling Eli on the first. Nothing had been said until the digging was finished, and Eli spoke to one of the men, "Did you see this happen?"

The man looked at Eli, glanced to the others, and asked, "You say some ting?" as he motioned to the graves. Eli knew he was talking about him saying something after the burial, but Eli shook his head and bent to grab the first body under the shoulders, nod to the others to take the feet and they lowered the body into the shallow grave. After placing the other, the four worked silently filling in the graves and rolling the rocks on top of the dirt mounds.

With shovel in hand, Eli went to the packhorse and replaced the shovel, turned, and was surprised to see one of the Chinese standing near, the others walking away. The man looked at Eli, glanced to the others, and said, "Yes, we see. Many men came, did this, put up sign, leave."

"Did the leader ride a sorrel horse, light mane and tail, white stocking feet. Big man?"

"Yes."

"Did they try to take your claim?"

"No. We knew they come. We stood with guns. We have more, they leave."

"You had more men and guns?" asked Eli, incredulous, as he frowned at the man. He had only seen four or five working when he passed their claim earlier.

"Yes, we work shifts." He held up one hand with all fingers extended, "Five men each shift, but we all there when they come. We have fought many battles. In our homeland, we are from Kwangtung Province where we fought in the Taiping Rebellion. We left there to get away from the fighting, but it still comes."

"If this bunch is who I think they are, they will probably come back. They want all the claims to do hydraulic mining. Do you know what that is?"

The Chinese man nodded, "We see in Cal'forn'a. Lot of water, wash dirt down, destroy. Seinfeld."

"Ummhmm," replied Eli. "That's what the sign says, so, watch yourselves."

"What you do?"

"Nothing with the goldfields, I'm looking for my

sons, twins." He spoke as he reached for the tintype and extended it to the man.

The man accepted the tintype, looked at Eli, "I am Chin Lee." He looked closely at the tintype and returned it to Eli, "I not see them."

Eli grinned, "I'm Eli McCain. Good to meet you, Chin Lee." He tucked away the tintype and reached out his hand to shake, "Remember, be careful, and don't trust that bunch."

Chin Lee nodded, accepted Eli's offered hand, and shook it. "We be careful. You be careful also," he stated, then added, "Zǒu ba, wǒde péngyǒu. Go in peace, my friend." He folded his hands at his waist and bowed slightly as Eli turned to mount.

———

THE MULLAN ROAD hugged the north edge of the valley, riding the low end of long sagebrush-covered shoulders that fell away from the rolling hills. He passed two more claims that appeared to be worked out and abandoned, both bearing stakes with signs declaring ownership by the Seinfeld Mining Company. The hills on the north side parted to show another small creek coming from high up and the signs of claims. With a glance downstream of the Daylight Creek, he turned Rusty's head to the north to take to the trail that sided the little creek, called Granite Creek. The tracks of several horses showed in the powdery dust of the trail that came from Granite Creek. Eli leaned down, looking at the tracks, but nothing unusual showed, although he was relieved to see them coming from the little creek bottom and turn to go downstream on the Daylight. These were fresh tracks, only a few hours old, and he suspected he would find other claims stolen.

The first claim at the mouth of the coulee appeared to be abandoned, the second claim also. But the third claim had been broken up and scattered about, two rockers had been smashed, and a small cabin with a sod roof had been burned, smoke still spiraling up in thin tendrils reaching for the sky. Two bodies showed, one beside the cabin, the second with legs protruding from the doorway. The stench of burning flesh wafted about, prompting Eli to lift his neckerchief over his mouth and nose. The horses were skittish at the smell of death and burning flesh and Eli backed them away from the scene of destruction.

The trail was on the north edge of the coulee, over-looking the creek and the valley bottom. Eli reined up, leaning on his pommel as he considered what he had found and what was happening. He looked down at the fresh tracks in the dust, saw what he thought was at least two horses sporting fresh shoes. He stepped down to examine the tracks, looking to both sides of the trail. He could make out the two horses had ridden with the bunch up the valley, but only one set had returned with the other riders. The rattle of distant gunfire brought him up to step into the stirrup and swing aboard the claybank stallion.

He dug heels as he slipped his Winchester from the scabbard, jacked a round into the chamber and lay the rifle across the pommel as he leaned into the wind. The trail dipped into the hillside and bent back toward the creek to rise onto a shoulder and disappear over the crest. Eli reined up and took to the ground at a run and dropped behind a big sage at the crest of the shoulder.

Just ahead and in the valley bottom, two men had

attacked a claim, riding headlong into the creek, but had been stopped by the return fire of two men, one belly down beside his rocker box, the other behind the pile of cast-off rocks. The two riders had dropped to the ground, using some scraggly willows and alders for cover, but rapidly firing at the two miners. The spaced-out shots and big booms of the miners' rifles told Eli they had Sharps single-shot rifles. Although good for hunting and distance shooting, they were outgunned by the attackers who both had repeaters. One of the attackers rose to run toward the creek bottom, was fired on by the miner, but dove headlong into the tall grass unharmed. The second man started his charge, splashing across the creek, and dove into the dirt bank, shielded from the miners.

Eli was too far away for accurate shooting and climbed back aboard the stallion as the gunfire continued. He slapped legs to the stallion and rode over the crest of the shoulder, charging toward the attack. The attackers did not see Eli's charge and as the one man rose from the grass, a bullet from Eli's Winchester nailed him to the ground. Eli swung the big horse toward the second shooter, but a bullet whipped past his head, and he dropped along the neck of Rusty, burying his face in the mane. He slid to the far side of his mount, dropped into the grass, and looked for the attacker.

The shooter rose, looked back toward Eli, and to the miners. He lifted his rifle for a shot at the miner by his rocker, but Eli's Winchester bucked and roared to send a .44-caliber bullet toward the target of the man's side under his arm, and it flew true to its aim, knocking the man to the side just as he pulled the trigger on his rifle. The rifle roared, the man screamed, and both ended up in the gravel at the edge of the creek.

Eli shouted, "Hey, you two! I'm friendly! Don't shoot!

I'm gettin' up!" He waited for a response, and said again, "I'm getting up and I'm holdin' my rifle high!" He slowly rose, holding the rifle with both hands high over his head. "I'm gonna put this back in the scabbard on my horse, then I'm comin' over!"

He moved slowly back to the waiting claybank and slipped the rifle into the scabbard. He grabbed the reins and started toward the creek, leading the big stallion and followed by the grey packhorse. Rusty tossed his head and snorted, looking toward the grass where the first attacker fell, and Eli saw movement. Eli slipped his Colt pistol from the holster, held it before him, dropped the reins to ground tie the stallion, and started toward the man at a crouch. A moan came from the grass, but Eli moved silently. As he neared, he said, "If you know what's good for you, you won't move!"

"Wha...who're you?" asked the figure still lying in the grass.

Eli moved closer, he stood at the downed man's feet and saw blood at the side of the man's head, his hand holding the wound and blood running through his fingers. "Where you at?" mumbled the shooter.

"I'm behind you. Now, get up slow and keep your hands where I can see 'em."

The man came to his hands and feet, struggled to stand and with hands held wide to the side, he stood, waiting, and started to turn back but was stopped when Eli said, "Move on across the creek, they're waitin' for you!"

# CHAPTER 9

## PAYBACK

"I thought we were waitin' on Knuckles an' Jonesy!?" asked Kelso, riding beside Karl Wolff, the leader of the gang.

"Ah, they're always late. I ain't worried about 'em, Knuckles can handle most anything. We've got more claims to take."

Kelso glanced at Wolff, glanced back at the others behind them, and back to Wolff. Kelso, for all his bluster and bravado, was afraid of Wolff, who was bigger and proven as a fighter with fists or weapons and as far as anyone knew, he had never been beaten. Kelso coughed, cleared his throat, and asked, "Not that I'm complainin', but didn't Seinfeld say he didn't want any killin'?"

"He said he wanted all the claims in the valley, and it was up to me how we'd get 'em." He growled his answer, looked at Kelso with squinted eyes, "He also gave me the money to buy 'em if we had to, but the way I see it, if we don't buy 'em, we keep the money," he chuckled, and let a sadistic grin split his face. He turned to look as they came unto another claim, the upper end showed signs of

being worked, but no one was there. He stood in his stirrups, looked further downstream toward what appeared
to be a long-tom and more, but several workers were
busy. He frowned, shaded his eyes from the midday sun,
and grumbled, "More Chinee! Consarn them slant-eyes!"
He settled in his seat, looked to Kelso, "If they're armed
like the last bunch, we need to go in shootin'!"

Kelso nodded as Wolff turned to face the others,
"More Chinee! We're goin' in shootin' so make your
shots count! I ain't gonna let this bunch run us off!"

Grumbles and nods came from the men as they
slipped rifles from scabbards and jacked rounds into the
chambers.

Wolff looked to Kelso, spoke loud enough for the
others to hear, "Kelso will take Zeke and PeeWee. Herb,
you'll come with me. We'll go across the crick, come at
'em from the far side. Kelso, you take the road, hit 'em
from this side." The others nodded and the gang split up.

———

ELI CROWDED the man before him, "Go on, cross the
creek!" he demanded, pistol in hand and leading his
horses behind him. They pushed through the willows,
splashed across the creek, the prisoner keeping hands
high, but stumbling and staggering, the head wound
bleeding down his cheek and neck. He called out to the
men at the claim, "We're comin' in! Don't shoot!"

"C'mon in but keep yore hands where I can see 'em!"

"Climb that bank and don't stumble, I might shoot
you just cuz!" ordered Eli.

As the whimpering man climbed the bank, he was
groaning and whining, put his one hand to his head and
moaned, but kept moving. The miner that had been by

his rocker was standing, rifle at his hip and finger on the trigger. The big Sharps looked like a cannon when it was aimed at you, and Eli cautioned, "You can point that cannon the other way if'n you don't mind."

"I ought just shoot you!" declared the miner. "You kilt muh partner!" He was glaring at the attacker with his hands held high, glanced to Eli, "Who're you?"

"Name's Eli. I was just passin' by, heard the shootin', came to help."

"Help who, them or us?"

Eli groaned, shook his head, "Do you really think that if you hit these two with your cannon this'n would still be breathin'? I shot this'n when he rose up from the grass, and I shot that'n just 'fore he dropped a hammer on you!"

The man stepped to the side to see Eli, who stood behind the wounded man. He looked at the man's head wound, frowned, looked back at Eli, then turned away to go to the other downed attacker. As he neared, he held his rifle on him, approached cautiously and when close enough he kicked at the man's hand but there was no movement. He poked him with the muzzle of his rifle, then stepped closer to look at the man's wound. The kill shot had entered the side under the man's uplifted arm, traveled all the way through his body and plowed a hole out the other side, taking bone and meat with it. The miner shook his head, "Yup, he's dead alright. He's a big'un too! And I guess it were yore shot what done it." He lowered his rifle as he walked back to the others.

"What about your partner?"

"He's dead. Took a bullet in the head. He was dead 'fore he hit the ground." He looked at the attacker, "What'd you come after us fer?"

"We was ordered to. If we didn't, they'd shoot us, too!"

"Who ordered you?" demanded Eli.

"Wolff an' Kelso," answered the man, who had sat down on a log, holding his head as he struggled to talk. "We was all...workin' fer...Seinfeld Mining. They's wantin' to...take this whole country and do that hydraulic mining stuff."

"What's your name, and what was that'ns name?" asked Eli, motioning to the dead man.

"I'm Jonesy, an...that's Knuckles. Don't know his real name."

Eli looked at the miner, "And your name?"

"Oh, I'm Smitty and muh partner's Joe Clark, uh, was Joe Clark." He shook his head, squinted at the one called Jonesy, and asked Eli, "What're we gonna do with him?"

"First, we make him dig a grave for your partner, then I might take him into town to the sheriff."

"That sheriff wouldn't know what to do with him, 'cept maybe feed him. He's as worthless as teets on a boar hog!"

Jonesy mumbled, lifted his head, and looked at his bloody hand, "I need some doctorin' 'fore I can do anything! You gotta get me to a doctor!"

"And just where we gonna find a doctor, even if we wanted to?" asked Smitty.

"Ain't there one in town?"

"Nope, and I wouldn't waste muh time goin' to get him anyway!" grumbled Smitty. "You go over there an' dip yore head in the crick, that'll help you more'n any doctor. Then you can come o'er here an' start diggin' a grave fer muh partner you kilt!"

Jonesy breathed heavily, struggled to stand and was a little wobbly on his feet, but made his way to the creek.

He dropped to his knees at water's edge and reached down to scoop water in his hands but did little good. He dropped to all fours, stuck his head in the water and sloshed about, then started to lift his head up and fell forward into the water, unmoving. Eli and Smitty looked, frowned, and Smitty said, "He ain't movin'!" He looked at Eli, back at the man in the water, and said, "We can't let him drown, can we?" and started to the creek.

He splashed into the water, grabbed the man by the scruff of his neck, and lifted. As the man's head came from the water, he had a big rock in his hand and swung it at Smitty, but the miner ducked and was hit with a glancing blow, but it staggered him back as Jonesy fought to his feet, looking at the miner and readying to swing the rock again, but Eli's pistol barked and spat, the bullet taking the man in the right shoulder, making him drop the rock and stumble forward onto his knees in the water.

Smitty stepped back, looked at the attacker, back to Eli, and again to Jonesy, still on his knees. Smitty walked over and put his foot on the man's back and pushed him face down into the water. He turned away and sloshed out of the creek, mumbling, "He can drown fer all I care!"

Eli stood on the bank, pistol in hand, a little tendril of smoke rising from the muzzle, and watched as Smitty fought against the water, pushed himself up and thrashed around, sitting on the gravel, water washing over his legs. He looked at Eli, "Well, help me outta here!"

"Get yourself out or drown!" growled Eli.

The water pushed against the man, red showing from the blood around him, and he fought to his feet and splashed out of the water, dropped on the gravelly bank and lay back. Eli looked at Smitty, "You watch him. I don't think he'll try anything else. He can't dig the grave, so I'll go catch up their horses and take him into town."

Smitty nodded, grabbed up his Sharps rifle, and sat on the rock they often used for their dinner table. He watched as Eli grabbed the reins of his big stallion and swung aboard. The grey, tethered to the flume, watched as Eli crossed the creek into the grassy meadow to catch the horses of the attackers. He soon returned to the miner's cabin and stepped down, glanced at Smitty, and looked to the creek bank where Jonesy still lay. He called out to the man, "You can either ride to town, or I'll put you belly down over your saddle and carry you into town. Which will it be?"

Jonesy lifted his one hand, struggled to his feet, and staggered to the horses. He looked at Eli, "You'll hafta help me up," and looked to his horse that stood waiting.

"Nope. Can't trust you. You get aboard, or I'll put you over!"

The man grumbled, went to his horse and stroked his neck, grabbed the stirrup with his left hand and turned it, reached for the saddle horn and with a hop or two, he pulled himself up and swung a leg over. Eli stood with the reins of the man's horse in hand, nodded, and handed the reins to Smitty. He stepped aboard the claybank, accepted the reins from Smitty, and nudged Rusty back toward the creek. He had thrown the lead of the grey over his neck and the packhorse knew he was free rein and pushed alongside the bay horse of Smitty and crossed the creek close behind the others.

It was midafternoon when Eli rode into Virginia City and straight to the sheriff's office. He pulled up before the hitchrail, called out through the open door to the sheriff, and stepped down. When he slapped the reins over the hitchrail, Sheriff Snyder stepped out, his thumbs hooked in his belt, and looked at the two before him. "Well, Eli, wasn't it?"

"That's right, Sheriff. And this," he turned to motion to his captive, "is Jonesy. He was with Kelso and Wolff. Him and his partner, Knuckles, attacked the claim of Smitty and Clark, and with a little help, Smitty's still standing, but Clark was killed by this man and his partner."

"Where's his partner?" asked the sheriff.

"That'd be Knuckles. He's layin' on the creek bank back to Smitty's claim. But he ain't goin' nowhere."

"He looks a mite bloody. He need a doctor?"

"I'd say he needs a rope. But you can fetch the doc if you want. I'm leavin' him in your hands."

Jonesy growled as Eli dragged him from the saddle, "You wait till Wolff an' Kelso get back. You won't be so proud o' yoresef' then!"

The sheriff heard what the man said and looked at Eli, "They comin' back to town?"

"Didn't see 'em anywhere."

The sheriff shook his head, grumbling as he ushered his prisoner into the jail, and Eli mounted up and started for the livery. He planned to talk to Liam and maybe see the youngsters, then he was planning on having a good meal and a good night's rest at the hotel.

# CHAPTER 10

## REPULSED

K elso turned and growled at Zeke and PeeWee, "Have yore rifles ready, we'll hit 'em hard an' fast! Don't want none of 'em grabbin' rifles an' such. Got it?" he glared at the two.

PeeWee, who fit his name, answered with his almost falsetto voice, "We gots it! We ain't no pilgrims!" He scowled at Kelso, his rifle in hand that made him look even smaller. The Henry had been cut down to fit him, the shorter stock and modified lever made it easy to fit his small frame and hands, but although small in stature, the measure of his meanness was far greater than his diminutive size. His lip curled and his nose wrinkled as his eyes glazed with hatred. He glanced to Zeke, the red-haired, red-bearded barrel of a man that was everything in stature that PeeWee was not, but Zeke was not the inherently evil man like PeeWee and the idea of attacking unsuspecting and unprepared Chinese didn't sit well, but he was needful of money and was willing to do whatever would be necessary to get his stake.

Kelso looked from one to the other, looked at the

sluice and flume at the claim, saw a few workers that were busy and barked the order, "Let's go!" He looked across the creek and saw Wolff and Herb Stein approaching from what they thought would be the blind side of the claim. Kelso stood tall, leaning into the charge as he kicked his roan to a run, he fired his pistol, even though they were not nearly close enough for a pistol shot. But it was a typical fault of those that let excitement overrule their thinking, and he fired again. PeeWee was on his left, Zeke on his right, and a sudden scream from the little man caught Kelso's attention. He glanced back over his shoulder, saw the fluttering feather at the end of an arrow that protruded from the chest of the little man and watched as he tumbled from his saddle. Kelso looked around—another arrow drove into the shoulder of Zeke. Kelso looked around frantically, and shouted, "Injuns!" and jerked hard on the reins of his roan, turning around and making for the road. He did not see Zeke but heard the thunder of hooves behind him.

They made the road and Kelso twisted around in his saddle, saw Zeke behind him, the shaft still protruding from his chest, but he did not slow. He was determined to get as far away from the Indians as he could. He frowned as he thought of Indians and realized he had not seen any, but he had heard that just because you can't see them, doesn't mean they aren't there.

———

WOLFF AND HERB started their charge after they saw Kelso and the others charging toward the claim workers. Wolff was a big man and handled his Spencer rifle almost like a pistol, holding it one handed against his shoulder and squeezing off his first round. The rifle bucked and roared, the smoke from the muzzle whiffing away as they charged at a run. He frowned as he saw the others across the creek turn away and run for the road, looked back at the claim and saw no workers, but the shout of Herb turned him, and he saw an arrow buried in the man's gut. Herb had pulled up on the reins of his mount, grabbed at the arrow and looked down as blood welled out over his hand and onto his saddle. He looked wide-eyed at Wolff, down at the arrow, and slid to the side and fell from his saddle.

Wolff looked at Herb, looked at the claim, and seeing no one, looked about frantically, pulled the head of his horse around and dug heels into the flaxen maned sorrel and lay low on the horse's neck as he made his retreat. The frown furrowed his brow and face as he kept his horse at a full run, splashed across the creek and made for the Mullan Road, headed back toward town. Dust rose from the hooves of the two horses that carried Kelso and Zeke, but there was nothing and no one behind him.

Kelso pulled up his roan to a canter, and back to a walk as Zeke pulled alongside. The feathered shaft trembled with every move of Zeke and the man looked at Kelso, "I gotta get this out! It's killin' me!"

Kelso looked at him, back down the road, saw dust that showed others were coming, and Kelso grabbed the reins of Zeke's horse and pulled him to the side. Kelso looked at the man, stared at the arrow, and said, "I can cut it off till we get to town, maybe to a doctor or somethin'."

Zeke looked at him and down at the arrow, "Do it!" Kelso slipped a knife from his boot and leaned over to start cutting on the shaft. Zeke held it tightly as Kelso cut, then broke the shaft.

"What'chu doin'?" demanded Wolff, who had ridden up when the two were busy with the arrow.

"Cuttin' the shaft. It was makin' the wound worse and he was whinin' about it!" answered Kelso, slipping the knife back into the scabbard in his boot.

"What happened to PeeWee?"

"He took an arrow too, but he was down an' I wasn't waitin'!" declared Kelso, reining his mount around. He looked at Wolff, "Where's Herb?"

"Same thing. Where'd them Injuns come from?"

"How would I know. Musta been hidin' with the Chinee or maybe they was just dressed like the Chinee, I dunno," answered Kelso, nudging his mount forward as the three started back to town.

"Did you see Knuckles and Jonesy?"

"Nope, din't see anybody, weren't lookin' neither," answered Kelso.

As they rode, they neared the claim of Chin Lee and the other Chinese that had repulsed them earlier, but they were only thinking about getting into town, getting some food and a room at the hotel. Suddenly a muffled blast, followed by another, startled the horses, and a massive cloud of black smoke boiled over the roadway and a horrible stench filled their nostrils. The men coughed, kicked their horses up to a canter, but could not see where they were going and pulled them back to a trot. Their eyes were burning, the stench was stifling, and the smoke impenetrable, and the horses were skittish, heads bobbing as they pulled at the reins and nervously sidestepped, snorting and coughing.

The rattle of what they thought was gunfire split the cloud of smoke and the horses started bucking and running, fighting the bits and twisting and bucking in their efforts to escape the melee. The three men dug deep in their saddles and stirrups, grabbing horns and reins, coughing and snorting snot and blood. Zeke was the first to be bucked off, but Wolff and Kelso held on a jump or two more, but when the horses reared up, pawing at the smoke, then buried their noses between their hooves and kicked at the clouds with their hind hooves, Kelso tumbled head over heels over the head of his roan, and Wolff soon followed.

The rattle of gunfire continued, and the men grabbed pistols from their holsters, stood back to back trying to penetrate the stinking smoke but saw nothing. Kelso started firing before him, seeing nothing but afraid of everything. Wolff also triggered his pistol until it clicked on an empty chamber.

Silence fell like a wet blanket, the black stench began to lift, and watery eyes squinted seeing nothing. Zeke was on his knees, Kelso on one knee, but Wolff stood, searching the wispy smoke for anything, but seeing nothing, tried to wipe it away from his face by waving his hands before him. "See anything?" he growled, his voice raspy.

Kelso responded, coughing, "No, nothin'!"

As the breeze lifted the smoke away, there was no one to be seen. On the ground at the side of the road were shattered pieces of pottery, black spread out like an explosion had occurred, and tiny bits of paper that fluttered in the breeze. What they didn't know was the pottery held stink bombs and the paper was from firecrackers, both used by the Chinese peasants in the Taiping Rebellion and the arrows came from the Tartar bows used by the peasants that fought in the same rebellion. The three men looked around, confused and stymied. Kelso started reloading his pistol with the cartridges from his belt and Wolff did the same, but it was all Zeke could do to get to his feet and holster his pistol with his left hand.

Without a word, the three men started walking toward town with nothing but a glance to the claim site where the Chinese had been that morning, but no one was to be seen. The men kept going, coughing and spitting, stumbling and mumbling, without talking to one another, keeping their pent-up anger to themselves. It had not been a good day for the gang.

————

ELI SAT at a table in the Miner's Café looking out the window as he sipped his coffee and saw three men, one he recognized as Kelso, walk down the street. One man had blood on his shoulder, but the others just wore their usual attitude, but streaks of black marked their faces and clothes and their boots were caked with a grey powder. Eli cocked one eyebrow up and shook his head. *Musta had a bad day.*

# CHAPTER 11

## QUESTIONS

"Have you had any word about your boys?" asked Liam, taking his seat at the head of the table, opposite Eli.

Eli watched the youngsters seating themselves, Eireann had already been seated by Liam. Eli pulled out his chair and as he seated himself, "No, nothing. Not a word. I'm beginning to think coming down this way was a fool's errand."

"But Eli..." began Christine, "if you hadn't come, where would we be? Probably dead!"

"Hold on there. Before we get into that, I think we should ask the Lord's blessing and give Him thanks for everything," stated Liam, looking around the table and taking his wife's hand in his right and Christine's in his left, nodding to the others to do the same. When everyone, including Eli, had joined hands, Liam began to pray. "Our Father in Heaven..." and continued to give thanks for the many blessings, the addition of the youngsters, and the company of Eli. He finished with an "Amen," which was echoed by the others.

Christine continued, "You can call it a fool's errand if you want, but I believe the good Lord sent you for us and I am mighty thankful for that. For a while there I was afraid the Indians were going to come back after us."

Narcissa and Jackson nodded, and stated in unison, "We are thankful for you, too!" as they smiled up at Eli.

"Alright, we're all very thankful. But we gave thanks to the Lord for this food, so how about we eat it!" declared a smiling Eireann, picking up the platter of thin-sliced turkey that had been bartered for by Liam just that morning.

Liam asked, "So, if you think they haven't been this way, what's next?"

"I haven't given it a lot of thought. I've talked to most of the merchants in town, several miners, prospectors, the sheriff, and others, but nothing. I was hopeful this would be the place I'd find 'em, but..." Eli shrugged. "Prob'ly head back toward Last Chance or thereabouts."

"I heard some fellas talking this morning about the new find in Bear Gulch. Maybe they got word of that and headed up there."

"Where 'bouts is that?" asked Eli, passing the platter of fried potatoes to Jackson, who grinned and accepted the platter and grabbed at the fork to dish some onto his plate.

"It's west of Helena, on the Mullan Road."

"I just hate to backtrack, seein's how I've already come south from Helena, hit the Bozeman Trail, and came on to Virginia City."

"You could always head west past Nevada City, on down through Fourteen Mile City, hit the Jefferson River, there's a trail on the west side that follows the river a bit, then...let me see...I think it's Fish Creek that comes from the west to hit the Jefferson, and there's a trail there that'll take you west and north. 'Bout the only thing up thataway is a new settlement I think they're callin' Butte. But just past there you can follow the Deer Lodge Creek up to Deer Lodge Valley and beyond."

"That's good to know, and I'll be givin' it some thought. That way I could go the rest of the way down Alder Gulch and beyond."

"So, you're leaving again, so soon?" asked Christine, sadness showing in her eyes.

"Yes, Christine, I'll be leaving in the morning, although right now I'm not sure exactly where I'll be going, but I've got to turn over every rock and hope the next one will show the boys."

Jackson frowned, "Are they under a rock?" His remark elicited the laughter of everyone, lightening the mood.

Eli chuckled, "That's just an expression, Jackson. What it means is I will have to do everything, look everywhere, and anything else I can do, to try to find the boys."

"We weren't hard to find," he responded, taking another forkful of turkey and jamming it into his mouth.

"Nope, and I'm glad I found you. But the way I remember it, you found me!"

Christine giggled and glanced at her aunt Eireann, "He was naked as a brand-new baby, too!"

Eireann's eyes widened as she put a napkin to her mouth and looked down the table to a very embarrassed Eli, whose face was showing red as he shook when he chuckled.

"That's right, I stunk so bad from diggin' in the dirt, I had to take a bath and didn't think anyone was anywhere around. I was sittin' on the bank, letting the sun dry me off when the animals spooked, and I grabbed my britches." He shook his head at the memory and grinned at the youngsters who were all giggling.

———

AFTER SUPPER, the men retired to the bench and rocker on the front porch, joined by Jackson, who thought himself a man. Liam was tamping tobacco into his pipe and looked at the boy, "Where's your pipe?"

Jackson frowned, "Uncle Liam, I don't have no pipe! I'm just a boy!"

"Oh, I thought since you were out here with the men, you were gonna smoke, too!"

Jackson looked from his uncle to Eli, "Eli's not smokin'!"

Eli chuckled, and replied, "Nope, haven't taken up the habit."

"So, I haven't taken up the habit either," declared the boy, folding his arms across his chest and giving an emphatic nod.

The men chuckled, and Eli leaned back, lifting the hot cup of coffee for a sip. Liam lit his pipe, gave a few puffs, and looked to Eli, "So, honestly now, what do you really think about your chances of finding your boys?"

Eli slowly shook his head, lifted his eyes to the golden sky, and answered, "I've had my hopes lifted and quashed, and right now, I just don't know. I believe the Lord will allow me to find them, I just hope it's sooner than later." He paused, looking down to the coffee and back to the western sky and the colors that seemed to be strutting across the horizon, changing from deep gold to bright orange and red, fading to a hint of pink. "I pray that I find them before anything bad happens."

The men continued to talk through the fading light of

dusk, discussing the many happenings in the world from the post-war changes to the prospecting and gold finds to the everyday humdrum happenings of a small town in a new territory. Liam also shared about the riderless horses that returned to the livery and the return of the two men that claimed them. He had overheard them talking about taking one man to the doctor and that he was still at the doctor's home. They also had spoken about others, but Liam could not make out what all was said.

As the light faded, they returned to the main room where the women were busy with teaching and learning needlepoint, but at the appearing of Jackson, Eireann stated, "Bedtime!" and the youngsters gave good-night kisses to all and disappeared. Eli bid his goodbyes and started back to the hotel.

———

THE SLOW-RISING sun was just beginning to make the low clouds in the eastern sky blush with pink as they announced the arrival of a new day. Eli glanced to the beginning colors that made dark shadows of the overlapping hills that held the morning light from its grand entrance. He pushed through the door of the Miner's Café and took a seat at the same table he had used the last time he visited. The pale light that showed faint color revealed all the fly specks and fingerprints on the window beside Eli's table, but his attention was focused on the slow filling cup of steaming coffee attended by a sleepy-eyed Micah. "Mornin'," he mumbled, "Egg'n taters?"

"That'll do fine," answered Eli, chuckling at the tired cook. "Bad night, Cooky?" he asked. The cook growled, sloshed some coffee on the table, but ignored it and turned away to the kitchen. Eli looked about, hoping to find a newspaper, but was disappointed. He looked out the window to see Sheriff Andrew Snyder step to the door of the café. When he entered, Eli motioned for the sheriff to join him and waved to Cooky to bring the coffee.

As the sheriff seated himself, he scowled at Eli, "You plannin' on bein' around here much longer?"

Eli frowned, "No, why?"

"Well, ever since you showed up, things have been happenin' to my peaceful little town and I don't like it!" he declared, nodding to Cooky as the man poured him some coffee.

The sheriff took a draught of coffee, set the cup down, and glowered at Eli, "First, you whip the town bully, and that was fine with me, don't get me wrong. But then you bring in one of the outlaws and say he killed a miner, and he just happens to be friends with Kelso. Now, I see him an' that one called Wolff come into town, afoot, with another wounded man and leave him at the doc's. Now, there's no tellin' what's gonna happen next! That's why I was hopin' you was leavin'!" He reached for his coffee for another drink as he looked at Eli over the rim of the cup.

"Well, Sheriff, I was just gonna have my breakfast, then I was plannin' on gettin' my horses and leavin'. How's that suit you?"

"Good."

"But I would like to talk to your prisoner before I go. I'd like to ask him about my boys." Eli reached for his cup and looked at the sheriff, "Have you heard anything about my boys?"

The sheriff frowned, shook his head, "Not a word. I

have asked around a mite, but everybody I asked said you had already been there."

Eli chuckled, "Well, Sheriff, for your trouble, how 'bout I buy your breakfast?"

"That'd suit me just fine!"

# CHAPTER 12

## RUN-IN

Eli and the sheriff had finished their breakfast and sat back to enjoy the coffee that was steaming in the tin cups before them. As Eli leaned forward to pick up his cup, movement outside the window caught his attention and he leaned back, twisted around a bit to see two familiar horses tethered at the hitchrail in front of the sheriff's office. Eli looked at the sheriff, "You expectin' comp'ny?"

The sheriff frowned, "What now?" he grumbled, pulling his coffee cup close to savor the aroma and warmth of the cup. He scowled at Eli, waiting for his answer.

"Looks like Wolff and Kelso just tied off in front of your office. Can't see them, but I recognize that flaxen maned sorrel of Wolff's, and the strawberry roan of Kelso's."

"Wal, the office is locked up, so they'll either hafta wait or come lookin'."

"I think they're waitin'," answered Eli, sipping his coffee.

The sheriff downed the rest of his coffee, pushed the cup away, and stood. He paused, looked at Eli, "You comin'?"

Eli grinned, nodded and stood to follow the sheriff out of the café. When the sheriff stepped down to the boardwalk, he glanced to the side and saw the two men waiting at the door of his office. He spoke to Eli over his shoulder, "They look a mite upset."

"I'm right behind you, Sheriff. You lead, I'll follow."

The sheriff grunted, hitched up his britches, ran his fingers through his long hair, and started toward his office. "Howdy, boys! What can I do fer ya?" he asked, as he reached for the key to open his office door.

The one known as Wolff glanced from the sheriff to Eli and back, "You've got a friend of ours in there. We're here to bail him out."

Kelso scowled at Eli, but as Wolff started to step up and into the office, Wolff turned to Kelso, "You wait out here, got it?"

"Yeah, sure. But what about him?" he pointed to Eli who was right behind the sheriff.

"Stay," he commanded, sounding more like a man correcting his dog than a partner. Kelso grumbled, turned away to lean against the front sill of the office window, and watched as the others stepped into the office.

The sheriff was talking as he walked around his desk to take his customary seat, "There ain't been no bail set yet. That's up to the judge an' he won't be in till, oh, 'bout ten."

Eli had stepped close to the potbellied stove that had a pot of cold coffee on it and grabbed the pot and turned to see Wolff grinning as he held his pistol on the sheriff. Wolff glared at Snyder, "Sheriff, drop your gun belt on the floor," he looked at Eli, swung the muzzle of the pistol toward him, "You too! Now!" he barked, stepping back a pace and looking into the cell. He spoke to Jonesy, "Hey in there, wake up! You're gettin' out!"

Eli sat the coffeepot back on the stove, turned to face Wolff, and reached down to unbuckle his gun belt. Wolff had positioned himself to see out the window as well as back to the cells and watch the two men. Eli, facing Wolff, dropped his gun belt, letting it hit the floor with a thud that caught Wolff's attention for a second. The gang leader grinned and looked at the sheriff, "You, get the keys and open the door!"

Wolff was watching the sheriff as he reached for the keys hanging on a peg in the corner and failed to see Eli's hand reaching for the LeMat behind his back under his vest. Wolff turned, was shocked to see the LeMat pistol in Eli's hand and froze. He looked at Eli, saw a wide grin as Eli softly spoke, "Now, you have a choice. You can drop that pistol and let the sheriff put you in the cell with Jonesy, or…"

The confidence of a big man that had never met his match, mainly because of his intimidating size, would seldom be tempered by a single incident. And a man like Wolff that had always bested anyone that stood before him, was not about to let this man back him down, especially since he held his pistol in hand and ready. All he had to do was swing it a little to the left, drop the hammer and the threat would be gone, but there was something about the cocky expression on the face of this man that grinned at him. But Wolff had never read any of Shakespeare and if he had he would not have paid any attention to the expression "Discretion is the better part of valor," nor would he have understood it.

Wolff made the move he had made many times before, dropping into a crouch to spin toward the target, but the blast of the LeMat pistol in the hand of Eli sent the lead into the side of Wolff's neck, and the second blast from the center barrel sounded louder and the shotgun pellets tore into Wolff's lower torso as the blast caught him just below the belt buckle.

Eli turned to the door expecting Kelso to crash in, and as the door slapped back, the big figure of the man filled the door, pistol in hand, making a target that could not be missed. Eli dropped the hammer on the LeMat once, twice, and the bullets took Kelso in the chest, burying the tag from the Bull Durham cigarette tobacco in the blood that blossomed at his shirt pocket. Eli had already cocked the hammer for another shot, but Kelso crumpled on his face, dropping his pistol, his leg making one spasmodic kick, and a groan from the man stilled the office.

Smoke from the shots filled the office, lying in grey layers, the acrid smell fouling the air. Eli looked from the sheriff to the bodies and back to the sheriff. "That might take care of some of your problems, Sheriff."

The sheriff coughed, dropped into his chair, and looked at Eli, "Like I said before, I'll be glad when yore gone!"

"Then I'll go talk to your prisoner, and you can send for the undertaker," stated Eli, bending to get his gun belt and strap it on. He went to the cells and looked at Jonesy, who asked, "What was all the shootin'?"

"Your partners tried to get you out without paying bail money."

Jonesy frowned, leaning to the side to try to see out into the outer office, but saw nothing but the wispy gun smoke. He looked back at Eli, "So, what'chu want?" he growled, backing away from the bars to sit on the bunk.

Eli dug out the tintype, held it for the man to see and

asked his usual questions, but the only response was, "I ain't seen nobody like 'at."

With a nod, Eli turned away and returned to the outer office. He saw the undertaker looking over the bodies. The man in the bent top hat and black coat looked at the sheriff, "So, who's payin'?"

"Look in their pockets, see if'n they got some money," suggested the sheriff. He looked up at Eli, "Ain't'chu gone yet?"

Eli chuckled and nodded, "You could probably sell those horses to bury 'em."

"Prob'ly. So, you goin' to Bear Gulch or Confederate?" asked the sheriff.

Eli grinned at the sheriff, reached across the desk to shake his hand, "I think I'll try Bear Gulch; it seems to be the hot spot now."

"See ya!"

Eli chuckled and turned on his heel and left the office.

————

IT WAS JUST shy of midmorning when Eli rode from Virginia City, headed west down Alder Gulch. He spent the rest of the day stopping at businesses, claims, and anyplace where there were more than two or three people, just to show the tintype and ask about his boys. He went through the many towns known collectively as Fourteen Mile City: Junction City, Adobe Town, Nevada City, Central City, Bear Town, Highland, Pine Grove, French Town, Hungry Hollow, and Summit. Although the only remnant of some of the once busy towns was often the empty stares from dark cabin windows, a few diehards remained in a few places, and he would stop and talk whenever someone would stop and listen.

By late afternoon he had passed through the remains of the many towns, ridden past the many claims, both working and abandoned, and put Alder Gulch behind him when he broke into the wide and lush valley of the Ruby River. He made one last stop at the mercantile in Laurin and spoke with Jean Baptiste Laurin, asking about his boys, "Ain't seen them, but I had some fellas in this mornin' that said Red Cloud is stirrin' up trouble. They was deserters from Carrington's outfit and bound for the goldfields. They said Red Cloud warned 'em, but Carrington didn't pay no 'tention."

Eli left the mercantile, shaking his head at the stubbornness of some military men. He crossed the Ruby River, found a campsite among the willows on the west bank, and quickly tended the animals and made a good camp. He built a small fire, broiled some strips of venison and with leftover cornmeal biscuits, made himself a meal. After finishing it off with coffee, he rolled in his blankets for a good night's rest, trusting the animals to keep watch.

# CHAPTER 13

## NORTH

The rattle of trace chains, the crack of bullwhips, and the shouts of mule skinners prompted the four riders to move to the side of the road and let the freighters pass. Eight wagons trudged past, each pulled by at least a six-up of mules, a couple with five teams, leaving a cloud of dust in their wake that forced Jubal and company to take to the flats and the grassy meadow to avoid the worst of the brown cloud. Two Moons looked at Jubal, "So, where'd they come from and where they goin'?"

"Prob'ly came from Fort Benton, got that load of freight from the riverboats, and maybe headed to Fort Walla Walla, Washington Territory. Maybe outfittin' some settlers." He had lifted his neckerchief to cover his mouth, as did the others. Joshua chimed in with, "Or they could be carryin' supplies to Bear Gulch! But this is the Mullan Road, and it goes all the way to Washington Territory!"

"I thought you were newcomers to this country, just

like us. How's come you know so much?" asked Black Eagle, frowning at Joshua.

"We came up from St. Louis on the riverboats, took a job with a freighter outfit out of Helena and Fort Benton."

"So, you were doin' that?" Black Eagle nodded to the freight wagons that were barely visible in the heavy dust cloud.

"Not here, but yeah, we did that for a while."

Jubal led off and the foursome stayed on the Mullan Road as it sided the Little Blackfoot River. The river valley was lush with greenery; cottonwoods stood tall overlooking the willows, alders, and underbrush that sided the river, while the valley bottom with its subirrigated grasslands invited all manner of wildlife to roam free. North-facing hills showed black with thick timber of pines, firs, and spruce, while the south-facing slopes were dimpled with piñon, juniper and cedar. Jubal searched the hills for game, they were in need of some fresh meat, but Two Moons spotted a young buck coming from the river and without a word, slipped his Henry from the scabbard and snapped off a quick shot that dropped the buck into the grass. He grinned at Jubal, "Fresh meat!"

They wasted little time in field dressing the buck, deboning the carcass and using the hide to make three bundles of meat, one for the pack mule, one each for both Two Moons and Black Eagle. When they took to the road again, they rode two by two, Jubal and Two Moons sided one another, while Joshua and Black Eagle followed with Joshua leading the pack mule. By midday the Mullan Road bent west as it rounded the point of hills where the Little Blackfoot merged with the Hellgate River, the river that would one day be called the Clark

Fork. The road sided the river, but with the meandering course of the Clark Fork, the road did it's best to keep to the shoulder of the low foothills overlooking the river bottom.

"Hey, don't you think it's time for us to broil up some of that venison and have some coffee," called Joshua.

Jubal glanced to Two Moons who nodded, and Jubal said, "We'll stop up yonder, down there by the water!"

They had just taken to the grass to go into the cotton-woods when the thunder of wheels caught their attention and a Concord coach pulled by a six-up of horses and with the lettering over the door that said *Overland Stage and Express* clattered past, kicking up more dust. Jubal muttered, "Too many people! Worse'n a big city!"

"From what the newspaper said, there a sight more up Bear Gulch already!" responded Joshua.

"That's what I'm afraid of," muttered Jubal, pushing through the brush to a clearing among the cottonwoods at river's edge.

———

LATE AFTERNOON SAW the valley narrow and the shoulders of the hills push in to make a bottleneck of the valley as the road kept to the south side of the Clark Fork River. What had been a sunny day with clear blue sky, saw clouds gather and show dark shoulders. The wind picked up and the men jammed their hats down tight and buttoned their jackets, turning up their collars, all in a vain effort to keep out the wind that whispered cold. Steep rocky hills robed in black timber stood off their left shoulder, while the tall cottonwoods at rivers edge bent with the wind and scolded passersby with the rattle of leaves. Grey skeletons of long-dead trees lifted bony branches to catch the wind and send it on with an eerie howl that foreshadowed the coming storm.

With one hand on the reins, the other holding onto his hat, Jubal hollered over his shoulder to his brother, "Josh! We might need to find some shelter! You doin' alright?"

"Yeah! I put some rocks in my pockets back yonder to hold me in the saddle!"

Jubal shook his head and glanced to Two Moons, who had struck a similar pose with his head ducked against the wind and his free hand holding his jacket closed. The dark clouds rumbled, taunting the travelers with the blue lightning that crackled and illumined the black bellies of the clouds. The rain came in like a screaming banshee, throwing the water in their faces, pelting the heads of the horses and within moments, horses, gear, and clothes were drenched. The horses plodded on, trusting their riders but struggling with every step as they leaned into the wind and rain.

The road bent around a point of a shoulder, turning south as it followed the river. Jubal saw the black of trees and gave a big wave to the others to follow him into the trees. They broke into the woods, had a brief respite from the wind but only enough to see they were not the only ones that had sought shelter in the trees. This was apparently a known campsite and the freighters had already laid claim, but one man who stood in the lee of a big wagon, waved them in, "There's room and cover enough, c'mon in!"

The eight wagons had been lined out in two columns of four wagons, leaving the space between for the mules and the men. A good-sized fire was blazing under a massive tarp that had been stretched across the space between the wagons and most of the men were gathered around. A big coffeepot that probably held a couple gallons was sitting by the fire, the long bail with a leather glove hanging. Most of the men had cups and were staring into the flames until the four newcomers stepped down and began stripping the gear from the horses to toss it under one of the wagons. The teamsters looked at the visitors and back to the flames, grumbling and complaining about the weather.

Jubal heard one of the men grumbling about their lack of meat and turned to Two Moons, speaking just loud enough for him to hear, "I think these are hungry men and we've got fresh meat. What say we share?"

"Suits me, there's plenty more where that'n came from!"

When they finished with the horses, Jubal walked to the fire with the big bundle of meat over his shoulder, looked at the men, and grinned, "Since you fellas were so good to share your camp with us, how's about we share some fresh meat with you!" as he dropped the bundle on the ground before him. The hide fell open and the big cuts of meat showed fresh in the firelight and the men's faces lit up with both hunger and delight. One man hollered, "Hey, Cooky! We got meat! Bring your fryin' pans!"

The man that summoned the cook dropped to one knee beside the meat, brought out his knife from his boot top, and began slicing off pieces. Within moments, the cook had plopped down three big frying pans and they were soon sizzling over the flames. The cook's helper had produced a bag of potatoes and started stuffing them into the edge of the coals. The aroma of fresh cooked steaks delighted the men who stood in a line, their backs to the storm to protect the fire and the food, smiling at their anticipated feast.

Plates had appeared and each man soon had a dinner with meat, potatoes, and more meat and potatoes, and everyone was smiling. Most had crawled under a wagon with their full plates and cups but faced the fire for its warmth. Jubal and company had found seats on some boxes dragged from a wagon, and were enjoying the hot coffee after they ate, but the crackle of lightning made everyone jump and mutter their surprise. The thunder groaned and muttered, throwing its weight around the narrow canyon, every roar and rumble echoing to multiply the sounds. The crack and crash of lightning told of nearby strikes and when sparks and fire blossomed atop the ridge behind them, every man came from under the wagons, some standing on hubs and rims to look high into the black timber, fearing the worst.

The black of the storm was magnified by the crashing of lightning and the clap of thunder. The wind howled and the rain pelted, and misery was dealt to man and beast. Everything and everywhere was drenched. The tarp over the fire sagged with the weight of water and the men had to push up with poles and sticks to dump the water off the ends, but the wind showed no mercy and the water that cascaded from the tarp was blown into the men that stood around the fire to shield their only warmth with their bodies.

The river that had always showed itself lazy and meandering, began to rumble and roar as the water-logged mountains shed the overflow and sent it cascading down what had been dry gullies and arroyos to merge with the Clark Fork River. Doubled in size and depth, the river fought shy of its banks and spread itself across the valley bottom, tearing trees from their roots, dragging debris from spring floods along, and swallowing anything in its path, living or dead.

That campsite was on the shoulder of the hill, but the water from the river began creeping closer and stretched out briny fingers through the trees, swallowing pine needles and twigs to feed the flood waters. Some of the men disappeared, finding refuge in the beds of the freight wagons and under the water-laden tarps that covered the cargo, but space was limited and most were gathered around the threatened fire that was rapidly devouring all the dry fuel. When the flames began to sputter with the windblown rain, some sought for more wood, but there was nothing to be found and hopeless eyes watched silently as the flames dwindled, and soon left nothing but a few glowing coals.

Jubal and company had found a spot in the lee of a rocky overhang. They were sheltered from the downpour and wind, but there was no fire and little enough space for all four, but they hunkered together, sitting side by side, legs drawn up, backs to the cliff face, and wet blankets covering them. Jubal looked at the others, what he could see in the dark, and shook his head. He pulled his hat down and hunkered under the blankets and sought sleep.

But sleep was not to come; a blast of lightning exploded near the camp as the fingers of blue drove the length of the tallest ponderosa, splitting it from tip to trunk, and shattering and scattering the splintered wood, branches, and pine needles across the encampment. Jagged blue fingers of lightning reached out to the nearby trees, sputtering and sizzling with electric fire that burnt the trees, the smoke mingling with the rain, but every momentary flame was quickly extinguished by the downpour.

The blast startled and spooked the mules, sending them braying, kicking, and bucking as they broke through the rope corral rigged for the camp. The tie downs for the tarp stretched across the span were ripped from the pegs and rocked the freightwagons when the mules stampeded through the trees. Men screamed, running from the blast but to they knew not where for the wet darkness wrapped around them like a stinking wet blanket.

The horses were the first thought of the four as the blast shook them out of their blankets. Jubal jumped to his feet and ran to the picket line where the horses were tied. The animals were wide-eyed, spooked, and pulling at the ties, but the halters and ropes held as Jubal and the others went to their horses, talking easy and reaching out to touch and calm them. The horses trembled as they were jittery and sidestepping but with the men near and talking, the animals began to settle down even with the ruckus coming from the rest of the camp.

Men were scurrying about, stomping out fires from split limbs and splintered tree branches. Confusion spread like a rampant virus, anger, fear and uncertainty worn like a wet shirt by every man among the muleskinners and teamsters. Darkness descended, the deluge enveloping every fire and obscuring any light from the heavens except for the retreating lightning that flashed fear into every mind and heart.

Jubal looked at the others, "Looks like they lost their mules. They're gonna be needin' some help gettin' them back."

"Yeah, but ain't nuthin' can be done till light!" answered Joshua.

"Don't mean nuthin' to us, does it?" replied Two Moons.

Jubal glanced from Joshua to Black Eagle, "Weren't

you thinkin' that we might try doin' somethin' besides goin' after gold?"

"Yeah, but..."

"We might pick up a stake fetchin' those mules for the freighters," suggested Jubal.

# CHAPTER 14

## LOOKING

Mule hunting was a good call by Jubal. Although not all the mules were returned, a couple had to be put down with broken legs, one had washed down the river, and a couple more could not be found, but the freighters were happy enough to reward the four with fifteen dollars each and a promise of a job on their return trip; even so, the four friends were determined to find out more about the strike up Bear Gulch. Another day's travel on the muddy Mullan Road brought the men to the wharf of the ferry at the bank of the Clark Fork opposite the trading post at Bearmouth.

The trading post stood above the mouth of Bear Gulch, high above the water level of any spring flood or cloudburst like had come the night before. The log building was new as evidenced by the raw cuts at the ends of the logs and the fresh sod on the roof. A man stood in the doorway, arms folded across his chest, as he looked at the newcomers that led their horses from the ferry to his trading post. "Howdy, gents! Welcome to

Bearmouth! If yore needin' some supplies, I've got 'em. C'mon in!" He turned away and moved into the cabin that was serving as a trading post.

Jubal was the first to step in, pausing to let his eyes become accustomed to the dim light and looked about to see shelves that lined three sides of the room, all stuffed full with a variety of goods, barrels of flour, cornmeal, and more stood along one wall, hand lettered signs indicating contents and prices. The wall on the left held a rack of assorted rifles and pistols that hung on pegs, and a table was spread with items of clothing. It was a well-stocked store and better than most in the city. The man stood behind the counter, leaned forward on his elbows, and said, "I'm John Lehsou an' this is my post. What can I do for you gentlemen?"

The other three crowded in behind Jubal and looking about muttered their surprise at the quantity of goods. Jubal began with, "We don't need much," he looked back at the others, "but we could use some cornmeal, sow belly, coffee, and some ammunition."

The trader grinned and began gathering the goods, glancing at the men, "Goin' prospectin'?"

"Mebbe, but at these prices, maybe we ought to be puttin' in a store!" mumbled Joshua, looking about and fingering some of the clothing.

"These are cheap compared to what you'll find up at Beartown!" declared Lehsou, finishing up the gathering of the goods and stacking it on the counter. When he gave the price, the men looked at one another and began digging into their recently acquired funds and shared the cost which took most of their money that they had acquired just that morning with a half-day's hard work.

Jubal chuckled as he pushed the paper and coin

across the counter, and said, "We might be better off just gettin' a job!"

"There are plenty to be had. I need some men to haul this morning's load up to Ten Mile Gulch to the packer, and Jimmy 'Clubfoot' Smith, the packer, is always lookin' for help. Course there's always work with the new mines and from what I hear, they're startin' to build some reservoirs to control the water for the sluices."

Joshua looked at his brother, "At least that way, we'll always be makin' money and won't be missin' too many meals!"

"At these prices, we'd hafta work two - three days, just to get 'nuff for one meal. And another two to three for you to get a meal!"

Two Moons and Black Eagle laughed, chided Joshua, and Two Moons said, "Reckon what yore brother's sayin' is he counts and you don't!"

"Yeah, that's the way he's always been, till he comes on a problem he can't solve then he comes lookin' for help!" mumbled Joshua, shaking his head as he grabbed a couple bundles and started to the pack mule. Jubal stayed behind, dickering with the trader about driving the wagons to Ten Mile Gulch. He shook hands, turned away, and walked out of the trading post, a broad grin splitting his face. He walked to the others, began doling out money, and chuckling, "See there! I got our money back and then some."

Joshua frowned, "What'd you do now?"

"Made a deal for us to load the wagons, drive 'em up to Ten Mile Gulch, and pass the word to the packer that might get us a job helpin' him pack the stuff the rest of the way to Beartown. How 'bout that!? We don't hafta pay for our goods, and we get paid to go to Bear Gulch and have money in our pockets when we get there!" He chuckled, looking at the others, pride in himself for what he had done and laughed as he started toward the stack of goods and the wagons.

The mouth of Bear Gulch was about three to four hundred yards wide, almost all gravel and even after the cloudburst of the night before, it appeared to be dry. The warm sunny morning had dried off the rocks and gravel, and the scattered alder and willows would suck up the rest of any remaining water. The mountains easily shed the water and any debris that had washed down the gulch had already been carried into the Clark Fork, and further up the gulch narrowed.

Four wagons were set to make the short journey up Bear Gulch to Ten Mile Gulch. "So, what're we gonna do with the wagons after we get there?" asked Two Moons.

Jubal chuckled, "First, we'll hafta unload 'em, then we'll leave 'em be. The trader, Lehsou, said he an' his helper'd come get 'em later. We'll just unhitch, tether the mules, and head on our way."

"Thought you said we might get on with the packer that'll be haulin' the rest of the way."

"Won't know that till we meet up with him. He might not need any help," answered Jubal, as he climbed up into the prairie schooner wagon. They had tied off their horses to the back of the wagons and would take the narrow road single file with Jubal in the lead.

Calling the trail a road was an insult to any self-respecting road for it was more of a two-track trail than a road, although it had been traveled by wagons before them. Although Lehsou had explained they would only go about four miles before unloading, it would be a challenging four miles. The hills on the left or west side were thick with fir, spruce, and pine, but the hills on the right showed as many rocks as trees and scattered bald spots that bore bunchgrass. The trail dipped across the gulch, taking to the easier slope on the north side, but the steep hill did little to accommodate the travelers, with the two ruts more often than not pitching the wagons at an uncomfortable angle on the side of the hill, prompting the drivers to brace themselves with one foot on the sideboards as they leaned far to the uphill side, all the while arguing with and encouraging the mules to keep the pace.

They had gone barely a mile when the gulch narrowed, the steep-sided hills pushing in with broad, unyielding shoulders, and forcing the trail to the gravelly bottom of the gulch. The footing was uncertain, but the mules dug in valiantly, bullwhips cracking over their heads, and as the trail took advantage of a slight shoulder, they rose out of the gulch bottom and kept to the trail, side angled though it was, on the north shoulder of the hills.

The wagons protested, creaking, groaning, and squealing all the way. The mules, as is typical of the animals, dug in and kept pulling, for the mule, when kept busy, is a hard worker. But when he is given slack or idleness, he can be the most recalcitrant of beasts. Four hours on the trail and passing of three other feeder gulches, finally brought the wagons to their destination at the mouth of Ten Mile Gulch.

Jubal spotted movement in the edge of the trees and watched as a man rose from a rocking chair, the only item of human occupation that showed, and with a crutch under one arm, he moved into the open and motioned for them to move the wagons further up the gulch to a bit of a flat just past the mouth of Ten Mile. The men pulled the wagons alongside one another, and Jubal jumped down to walk to the back and meet the man he had been told was Jimmy "Clubfoot" Smith. Jimmy grinned as Jubal came around the tail of his wagon, his hand extended, as Jubal said, "I'm Jubal Paine, that'n," motioning to Joshua, "is my brother, Joshua, and those two are Two Moons and Black Eagle."

The other three came near and shook hands, as Jubal said, "Fellas, this is Jimmy Smith." He turned to look at Jimmy, "John Lehsou said you might could use some help with your packtrain up to the goldfields, that right?"

Jimmy frowned, looked over the four eager young men, and back to Jubal, "Any experience with pack mules?"

"Not a long train of 'em, but we've handled mules before. We have our own pack mule and we've handled them pullin' freighters and such."

Jimmy turned a critical eye to the four, lingering on the two Comanche, and asked, "What tribe?"

Two Moons grinned, "We're Numunuu or what you call Comanche."

Jimmy nodded, frowning, "Well, I reckon that's alright. Long's you're not any of Red Cloud's Sioux that's making war on everybody else, including other tribes, like the Crow and Blackfoot."

Two Moons nodded, "We were raised by a white man on his ranch in Texas. Made a cattle drive comin' to Montana Territory and now we're thinkin' about tryin' for gold."

"Ain't everybody? But the smart ones like me, make better money off'a all them poor fools diggin' in the dirt and gettin' nothin' but blisters and empty pockets." He glanced at the others, and then to Jubal, "I reckon I can use you. You've got your own horses?"

"Yessir."

"Good. I usually run about two hundred mules. With

five of us, we can each take forty so it might be easy 'nuff ."

The four looked at each other, then to Jimmy, as Joshua asked, "Each of us take *forty* mules?"

"Forty loaded mules. That's right. But they're used to the trail and follow along easy 'nuff. It's only 'bout six miles up to the end of Bear Gulch where the miners'll be waitin'. We can load 'em in the mornin', course I already have a stack of loaded panniers from the last wagons, and should make it by, oh, midafternoon." He looked at the four again, then nodded toward the trees, "Might wanna make a camp in the trees yonder. Get you sumpin' to eat and get some sleep. We'll start loadin' at first light!" He turned away and went to where they had seen his rocker but disappeared into the trees.

# CHAPTER 15

## CHANGE

Always wary of trouble from any source, Eli now traveled with a heightened awareness of Indian troubles. With the recent news about Red Cloud and his ongoing fight over the Bozeman Trail and the military building forts, he also knew the Sioux chief was allies with the Cheyenne, Arapaho, and even some of the longtime enemies of the Sioux—the Crow. He knew he was in the traditional lands of the Blackfeet, but he also knew they often had their own way of dealing with the encroachment of gold-hungry white men. Although he had been friendly with one of the Piikani chiefs, Running Rabbit, and the woman, Morning Dove, there was no way of knowing what band or even what tribe might be hunting in these hills.

Black timber-clad mountains rose high off his left flank, mountains that some were calling the Ruby Range because of the Ruby River Valley that meandered in the afternoon shade of the tall mountains. On his right, the mountains were more distant, and the rolling foothills held little promise of anything but disappointment whether hunting game or gold. But the valley of the river was lush and plentiful with game. Deer were abundant, elk were skittish but present, and a variety of small game from rabbits to coyotes and other predator types. As he neared the northernmost point of the Ruby Range, a wide alluvial plain stretched sandy fingers toward the grassy flat, the buff-colored soil and grasses standing in stark contrast to the heavy skirts of black timber on the mountains.

About an hour from the Laurin trading post, Eli passed a sign, *Sheridan,* that pointed to the east to another little settlement. He had heard talk about the town that had become the sawmill of the valley that provided lumber and timbers for homes, businesses, and underground mining throughout the valley and the many towns of what was known as Fourteen Mile City along Alder Gulch. The town would just be coming awake when Eli rode past and with so little activity and few people, if there were any left, he chose to keep moving. Disappointed too often by his failure to find anyone that had seen his boys, he chose to keep moving to get to the new gold find that suggested a little more hope.

The trail sided the Ruby River, a river that had more twists and turns than a den full of rattlesnakes, but the trail stayed straight, keeping the wide alluvial plain on the left and the grassy meadow on the right. When the lowering sun began making long shadows and a wide flat-topped mesa showed nothing but its own silhouette, Eli began looking for a campsite. A glance to the dark-ening sky showed boiling thunderclouds and the wind was kicking up, pushing dust into his face. But the threat of a storm and no shelter, made him focus his search. His attention was arrested by a fork in the trail with a sign that pointed west, *Rattlesnake Ranch.* About a hundred yards down that trail, he could see a barn, house, corrals, and a few more structures. With nothing else showing, he turned up the trail, hoping for at least a haymow in the barn for cover. It was always customary for settlers and ranchers to offer shelter to passersby, especially when a storm was brewing. As he neared, he saw a Concord stage with a six-up team preparing to leave. The jehu, or driver, was leaning down and talking to a passenger that was stepping into the stage, but hung on the door as he talked. The hostler was standing at the head of the team, holding the bridle of one of the lead pair keeping it steady until the driver was ready. A woman stood in the doorway of the house, watching the commotion, wringing her hands in her apron as the driver lifted his whip, waved to the house, and cracked the whip over the team and hauled back on the lines to turn the stage about and head back down the long road to finish his journey. The big stage rocked back on its thoroughbraces and with a creak of the axles and groan of the wheels, it kicked up some dust to wave goodbye to the station.

Eli moved to the side of the roadway, nodded to the driver and messenger as they passed, and waved away the dust once they were gone. He nudged Rusty forward, rode up to the house, and spoke to the woman who was still standing in the doorway, "Evenin' ma'am," as he tipped his hat, "Wonderin' if you'd mind if I put my horses in your barn, maybe spread my soogan in the haymow and get outta the weather?"

"Certainly. But have you had your dinner?" she asked, shading her eyes with her hand as she looked at the stranger on the big horse.

"No, ma'am, been travelin'."

"Well, I have plenty left after the stage. They didn't

have as many passengers as usual, and I made a big pot of stew. You're welcome, if you're of a mind."

"Thank you, ma'am. I'd be right proud to partake of your kind hospitality. Mind if I tend to my horses first?"

"You go right ahead. I'll get your plate ready." She dropped her hand, grabbed her skirt and apron, and turned about to go into the house. Eli noted she was a middle-aged woman, but attractive still. Her dark hair was done up in a bun at the back of her head, but her figure was not hidden by the long dress nor apron. He grinned as he reined Rusty around and headed for the barn. The wind was kicking up and a dust devil danced down the roadway. Eli had to grab his hat as a gust threatened to take it away. With head ducked into his collar and leaning low on Rusty's neck, he moved into the open door of the barn and stepped down.

He spotted an empty stall, led Rusty into it, and put the grey in the next stall. After stripping the gear, he gave them both a good rubdown, spotted a bin with corn and gave both animals a good scoop. Satisfied, he started for the house but stopped when something caught his eye and looked at the other horses in the stalls. There were three horses that had been ridden hard, not rubbed down and the sweat marks from saddles were still slick and matted. The animals had shown lather but were enjoying the hay in the troughs. The saddles and tack hung on the fencing, scabbards were empty of the rifles, and the bedrolls and saddlebags were nowhere to be seen. Eli frowned, he knew it was common for the stage teams to be in the corrals, but most riders would take better care of their animals.

He had stacked his gear at the front end of the stalls, knowing the horses would not allow any strangers in the stalls. He started for the house, pulled the big barn doors closed, and crossed the short distance, holding his hat on against the wind, and after a quick knock, pushed the door open to enter the house. Four men were at the table, a long table that would easily accommodate eight or ten, and the woman was refilling the coffee cups. All the men looked up at Eli but returned their attention to their plates. The woman turned, "By the way, I'm Phoebe Lowe," she nodded to one of the men at the end of the table, a colored man, "he is the hostler for the stages and our ranch worker, Eustis Higgins. My husband, Dermot, will be back soon. He went into Sheridan for some supplies." She made no attempt to introduce the others, but smiled at Eli and motioned him to the opposite end of the table.

He had no sooner seated himself than Phoebe put a filled plate and cup before him, and said, "If you need more, just ask. There's plenty."

He looked down to see a big helping of stew with meat, potatoes, carrots, onions, and a thick gravy. At the side were two fluffy biscuits and steam rose from the coffee cup. He turned to Phoebe, "Looks and smells wonderful, thank you!"

She smiled and nodded, "You're quite welcome. Enjoy." She turned away and disappeared into the kitchen. The others were hunkered over their plates and busy with the food, and a quick glance showed they were neither clean nor mannerly, just hungry. When Phoebe offered more biscuits, everyone, including Eli, eagerly accepted. Eli commented, "Those are the best biscuits I've had in I don't know how long!"

Phoebe smiled, "Thank you, sir," and went back into the kitchen area to retrieve the big pot of stew and brought it out for additional servings, which the men gladly accepted but the only one that expressed his

thanks was Eli. He glanced at the others with an expec-
tant look trying to goad them to say thanks as well, but
his actions went unnoticed. When Phoebe was finished
serving, she retrieved the coffeepot and began refilling
the cups. When she neared the three that were seated
with the hostler, one of the men leaned back, sneering,
and said, "You want comp'ny till your husband gets
back?" and dropped one hand to his side between his
chair and Phoebe as she stood pouring coffee from the
big pot, holding the bail and the handle with thick
potholders.

She did not even look at the man, but asked the
group, "Have you ever seen what a man looks like when
he has been scalded with a pot full of steaming coffee?"
As the men glanced to the brazen speaker, and back to
the woman, she continued pouring the coffee, the steam
rising with a taunting twist but a stern reminder of her
warning.

The man growled and mumbled, "Din't mean no
harm. Just thot'chu might be lonely."

Phoebe moved nearer Eli, offered the coffee with a lift
of the pot and a questioning expression. Eli nodded,
lifted his cup for her to fill and with her back to the
others, she whispered, "Please don't leave me alone with
them." She looked at him with wide eyes that showed
fear.

Eli smiled and nodded, "Thank you, ma'am. That has
been a fine meal." He glanced at the others and spoke to
Phoebe as she stepped behind him toward the entry to
the kitchen, "Ma'am, I know it's the custom for stage
stations to charge for the meals, but you haven't said
anything. Do you have a price, or an offering plate where
all of us can leave our payment?" Eli looked at the men
and the hackles on his neck rose, warning him of trouble.

The brazen one at the end of the table was a hatchet-faced man with narrow eyes, a hawkish nose, and splotchy whiskers under his dark, greasy-looking hair and thick eyebrows. The man to his left was an average-sized man with dirty blonde hair, looked to be in his late twenties, bony and lanky, gaunt faced with few whiskers but long hair that hung over his ears and collar. His eyes were constantly moving as if he was fearful of everything. The man to the right of the end of the table was bigger, bulbous red nose that was in stark contrast to the thick eyebrows and beard that were coal black. His hair hung long on the sides and framed his bald pate that showed a massive scar; Eli knew this man had been scalped. The long scar on his cheek showed white amidst the black whiskers and his heavy wool shirt was almost as black as his beard but with dirt and grease.

A wily grin split the face of the brazen one as he chuckled, looking to his two companions, "He thinks we oughta pay the woman!" and cackled as the other two joined him in raucous laughter. When they stilled somewhat, the speaker looked to the skinny one on his left, "Whatchu think, Willy?"

Willy laughed, "I ain't got no money to pay nobody nuthin'!"

"How 'bout'chu, Gad?" as he looked at the fat one.

The burly beast in black just grunted, snarled as he turned to Eli, "I think we oughta have her for dessert!"

"Whooeee! I do believe you got'chu a right fine idee there, Gad." He turned to face Willy, and asked, "Don'tchu think so, Willy?"

"I shore do, George. I shore do!" he answered and laughed as he looked at Eli and Phoebe who stood behind him. "Sides, she was a little too uppity to suit me, you know, when she threatened to scald you with that coffee!"

Eli heard the click of a hammer under the table and looked at George, who was cackling and watching Eli. George growled, "Stand up there, pilgrim, and open that there jacket an' lemme see what'chu got." As Eli stood, George growled at Eustis, "You! Git o'er there wit' them!" The hostler nodded, lifted his hands high, and scooted down the bench, eyes showing more white and fear, as he mumbled, "Yessuh, yessuh, I'se a goin'."

Eli stood, opened his coat to show the holstered Colt and the sheathed Bowie knife. George growled, "Woman! Get that there pistol outta his holster and that knife and put 'em on the table!"

Phoebe muttered behind Eli, "Should I?"

Eli nodded, still holding the coat open, and stood while she slipped the Colt and the Bowie knife out and lay them on the table. George growled, "Now, slide 'em down thisaway."

Phoebe looked up at Eli who gave a slight nod and reached down to slide the weapons toward the men at the end of the table. She stopped about half way, stepped back, and motioned for the blonde man, Willy, to get them.

George nodded to Willy, stood, and pushed back the bench he was sitting on and showed the pistol with a wave at Eli, "Now, put'chur money on the table."

Eli chuckled, "Ain't got much," and began to reach into his pocket with his right hand, holding the edge of the pocket with his left. He brought out a few coins, lay them on the table, and did the same with his left pocket and brought out some folded paper currency and lay it on the table. George saw the currency and let a slow grin split his face, "Now, that's better. You was wantin' to give her some money, she can have that little bit there," motioning to the few coins.

Eli nodded to Phoebe, motioned to the coins, and she stepped closer to scoop the coins off the table. As she did, Eli motioned for her to step back away from the table. He looked at George, frowned, "I meant to ask you. If you were to die today, do you think you'd go to Heaven?"

George frowned, glanced to his partners, laughed, looked back at Eli, "I don't believe in no Heaven."

"Oh, so that means you'll be going to Hell then?"

George frowned, "What're you, a preacher or sumpin'?"

"No, I'm just concerned about my fellow man and where you'll be going right soon."

"The only thing I'm concerned about is your money and that woman!"

Eli nodded, "Oh, I see. Well, I've also got some money in my wallet, do you want me to get it?"

"Why shore! We want it all!" he laughed, looking from Willy to a slobbering Gad who was leering at Phoebe.

Eli nodded, doing his best to appear afraid and nervous and reached to his back as if going for a wallet and slipped the LeMat from his waist and lowered it behind him. He coughed and covered his mouth with his left hand, using the sound and movement to cover the sound of cocking the hammer. He straightened up and moved his right arm as if bringing around the wallet but brought the LeMat to bear on George. He shouted as he did, "Drop it!"

But George's anger flared, and he lifted his pistol to shoot, but Eli's LeMat pistol belched flame, smoke, and lead. The bullet bore into the man's upper chest, driving him back a step, but George was still lifting his pistol and Eli fired again. The second bullet took George in the base of his throat, blossomed red, and tore out the back of his neck.

At the shout of Eli, Gad roared and clambered to his feet, knocking the table aside and reaching for his pistol buried in his bulk at his waist, but Eli's third shot hit Gad in the back of his hand and tore through his meaty mitt and into his belly. But Gad was only angered and fought his own jacket, tearing it aside to grab his pistol with his left hand just as another bullet from the LeMat plowed into his chest. He turned in a rage, blood showing in his eyes as he growled like a grizzly bear and knocked aside the long bench, stomping it with his clod-hopper boots, and took the next bullet in his shoulder. Eli fired again and the bullet tore into Gad's throat and ripped out the side of his neck. Gad put his meaty paw at his neck, looked at it covered in blood, and tried to roar again, but only spat blood. He kicked at the bench, stumbled, staggered, and fell on his face. The thud on the floor rattled dishes on the counter.

Eli turned to Willy, who stood grinning, "I counted 'em, you're empty!" he laughed as he reached for Eli's Colt that lay on the table. "Now, I'm gonna shoot you with your own gun, and I'm gonna have her for dessert, just like Gad wanted."

Eli chuckled, "Six shots?"

Willy nodded, grinning broadly as he grabbed the Colt. He was in no hurry, believing he had all the aces in the deck, but Eli cocked the hammer of the LeMat again, fired the bullet into Willy's arm, and the blonde bad boy jumped back, grabbing his shattered wrist, his eyes wide and fear painting his face. Eli said, "This is a LeMat pistol. It's sometimes called a Grapeshot Pistol, because it has nine bullets, and it's also a shotgun with grapeshot. Wanna see?" As he talked, he had flipped the lever on the hammer and pulled the trigger. The pistol bucked, barked, and spat a fistful of grapeshot pellets that tore into the chest of the braggart blonde as it drove him back against the wall. He slid down the wall, looked down at his chest and saw a bloody shirt and ripped open chest. Blood bubbled as he tried to breathe his last. He looked at Eli, fear on his face, and his head dropped to the side, sightless eyes seeing nothing.

Silence fell over the room that was filled with gun smoke and the smell of death. Eli slipped the LeMat back behind his belt, walked to the end of the table, and retrieved his Colt and the Bowie knife, put them away, and turned to Phoebe. "Sorry for the mess. Couldn't help it, they gave me no choice."

Phoebe sat down in the chair and dropped her face in her hands and sobbed. Eli motioned for Eustis to help him and grabbed the shoulders of Willy's jacket and started dragging him out of the room. Eustis picked up the man's feet and helped Eli. The rain had started, and the wind was howling, but he was sure the would-be road agents would not mind. They returned and did the same with George but struggled a mite with Gad. When the three were lined up outside, he went through their pockets and found that Gad was Augustus "Gad" Moore, George was George Ives, and Willy was William Page.

He held on to his hat and ducked his head into the wind as he pulled open the screen door and pushed into the house, followed closely by Eustis. He stood a moment, thinking and remembering, and remembered these were names of men that had been a part of the Plummer Gang that had been wiped out by the Vigilantes, but these and a few others had been banished instead of hung. He shook his head and chuckled, looked up to find Phoebe mopping the plank floor and trying to straighten up the furniture. She looked at Eli, "Thank you. I..." she shook her head and dropped into the chair, staring at the floor.

Eli motioned to Eustis and the two men quickly put the room back in order. He looked at the woman, "I just can't abide bad manners."

# CHAPTER 16

## DOWNRIVER

The wind whistled through the cracks, rattled the shutters, and made the smoke from the chimney occasionally backtrack. But the fire in the fireplace dispelled the cold that came with the deluge, and the shelter of the ranch house, though not totally weatherproof, was appreciated by Eli and Phoebe. They sat at the table nursing cups of steaming coffee, as Phoebe explained, "When Bill Bunton was hanged by the Vigilantes, his ranch was seized by the new Chief Justice, Hezekiah Hosmer, a cousin of my husband. We bought the ranch, but it took all we had, so when we were offered to take on the duties of stage station for the A.J. Oliver company, we took it. The extra money has helped, but I guess that's why those men stopped here. When they rode up, they asked for Bunton, all I said was he no longer owned the ranch. Then the stage came, and, well, you came…" she shrugged. She sipped her coffee, looked up at Eli, "And I am very glad you came."

"What about your husband, wasn't he due back before now?" asked Eli.

"Yes, he was, but he might have stayed over because of the storm. He would have thought I would be alright, what with stages stopping and Eustis helping."

Eli frowned and looked around, "Where'd he go?"

Phoebe laughed, "That's the way he is, quiet and easygoing. Sometimes I think he could sneak up on an Indian war party. He went to the barn. He has a room there; it's part of the tack room."

The wind cut loose with a long, lonesome howl that rattled some of the loose shakes on the roof and more, making Eli look about, wondering if the building could withstand the storm, but the wind abated, and the storm weakened to a constant downpour. Eli finished his coffee and stood, "Reckon I better go to the barn myself."

"Oh no, don't. I'll get some blankets and make you a pallet in here. You'll be soaked before you make it to the barn and it'll take all night for you to dry off, if ever!"

"But..." he began, only to be interrupted by Phoebe.

"No excuses. It's the least I can do for what you've done. Besides, I would feel a lot safer with you in here. What if some of their friends were to come in the night?"

Eli slowly shook his head, "I don't think anybody will be out prowling in this weather."

———

ELI WAS LEADING his horses from the barn in the grey light of early morning when a lone rider came down the roadway. Eli watched him as he rode to the barn, swung down from his mount, but watched as Eli slapped reins over the hitchrail in front of the house. When the man untied a big bundle from behind the cantle of his saddle, Eli guessed this was Phoebe's husband, Dermot. Eli nodded, went to the door and pushed it open, calling out Phoebe, "I think your husband's home!"

"Oh good, I did want him to meet you. You will stay for breakfast, won't you?"

"Planned on it." Eli turned back and went to stand in the door as Dermot came from the barn. He saw that Dermot was frowning, looking sternly at Eli as he swung the bag of goods over his shoulder. As he approached, he kept his eyes on Eli until he glanced to see the three bodies laid out in front of the small porch on the house. He frowned as he stepped closer to look at the three and looked up at Eli, "You do this?" he growled. "Where's my wife!" he demanded as he stepped closer. Eli moved aside, motioned into the house, as Phoebe called out, "I'm in here, Derm!"

The man made the steps in one long stride and slapped the screen door aside and stepped into the house. "You alright?" he asked, a mixture of emotions trembling his question.

"I'm fine, fine. Breakfast is about ready!" she turned and held out her arms for him. He stepped close, dropped the bag, and pulled her close as they embraced.

He leaned back, hands still at her waist as he looked at her somberly, "What happened?"

Phoebe smiled, "It'll take some tellin'. You wash up for breakfast and we'll talk over the meal."

———

PHOEBE SPENT MORE time talking than eating, explaining everything in great detail, a story that could have been told by Eli in a quick moment. When she finished, "So, now you know why I want my own pistol!"

Eli was surprised at the remark about a pistol, but

looked from Phoebe to her husband and back, refusing to become involved in the conversation. Dermot kept eating, listening to all she had to say, and when she paused, he pointed to the bag with his fork, and said, "Look in there," and continued eating.

Phoebe frowned, looked from her husband to the bag that sat by the counter, and back. She rose, stepped to the bag, and bent down to rummage through it, setting the contents, one after another, on the counter. As she reached the bottom of the bag, a flat box was brought out and she sat it on the counter, opened it, and squealed! "You did! You got me a pistol!" and pulled the small revolver from the box, hefting it in her hand, smiling and lifting it to point it out the window, closing her off eye and sighting down the barrel to line up the sights. It was evident she knew a little about pistols and dropped her hand, turned with a broad smile and went to Dermot's side, bent to hug him, and whispered in his ear, "Thank you, thank you, thank you. I love you!" She straightened up, smiling, looking at her pistol. It was a .38-caliber Colt pocket pistol, just her size. She glanced to Eli, back to her husband, and smiled as she sat back down at the table, laying the pistol beside her plate.

Dermot said, "I'll make you a holster for that. It'll be one that can hide behind your apron."

He looked at Eli, shook his head, "I didn't wanna do it. Said she didn't need one, but after what happened, I reckon she was right and I'm glad I got it."

Eli looked at his cup, lifted it to take a sip, and sat it down. "But that's just the beginning. You'll have to work with her until she's comfortable and confident. If not, she'll do more harm than good, but if she's comfortable with it," he paused, chuckled, "she'll be dangerous!"

All three laughed as Eli cocked his head to the side,

chuckling and reaching for his cup. He pushed back his chair and stood, reached for his hat, and said, "It's been good to get to know you folks. With a bit of work, you'll make a nice home here and you're just what this country needs. May the Lord bless you abundantly until we meet again!"

———

THE USUAL LAZY dog lay on the short boardwalk that stretched from the saloon to the General Store, both businesses bearing the name of Lott. A screen door slammed, and the creak of a water pump could be heard somewhere, but the grey bones of hitchrails were empty, and the rocking chairs in front of the store were idle. One man sat on the boardwalk beside the dog, looking just as lazy and sleepy as the mutt, but he lay a hand on the dog's head and was rewarded by an uplifted eyebrow. Eli chuckled to himself and kept moving, choosing to use the time he had to cover more ground. The little settlement did not sport a name, but the main landmark was a recently completed bridge over the Beaverhead River.

Here the Ruby River merged with the Beaverhead, Big Hole, and Jefferson Rivers and the wide valley was lush with grasses, trees, berry bushes, and more. It was a stark contrast to the browns, buffs, and pale tans of the dry land that held cactus and sage in abundance, and it was a cooler land to travel through. The valley that had been wide at the confluence of the rivers, now narrowed to a flatland of fertile greenery. He had crossed the Ruby River, taking to the trail between the Jefferson and the eastern flats.

The green of the valley narrowed to less than a mile wide, but the valley that included the wide alluvial plains that had fanned out over the eons of time stretched like the wide skirts of Mexican women dancers doing the Folklorico when they dropped to the floor at the end of the dance with wide skirts spread out before them. Eli followed a trail of the ancients, probably traveled in years long past by the Natives, even those that came before the Blackfoot, Crow, and Lakota.

The occasional ravine still showed water from the rain the night before, but most were already drying from the warm summer sun that hung high overhead in the cloudless sky. Eli, ever the student of God's creation, looked at the nearby bluffs that showed the erosion caused by the swift running river in the valley. The alluvial plains had stretched to the river, but the waters continually eroded the progress of the plains and kept the adobe bluffs trimmed to allow the green of the valley to provide for the abundance of wildlife.

It was nearing midday when the valley made a slight bend easterly and pointed toward the black hills that were marching in formation toward the river. The battalion of thick timbered mountains marched continually northward on a course that would intersect with the river. In the distance, taller mountains were shrouded in clouds and a rainstorm crowned the peaks. The trail, now crowded closer to the river, pointed to the water where the river was split by two islands, each offering shallow water to make a crossing.

Eli kept to the trail, pushed Rusty to the edge of the water, and nudged the long-legged red dun into the water. The horse dropped his nose, took a step and another, and walked in nonchalantly, his footing solid on the gravelly bottom. He stepped up onto the first island, across more water, the second island and two steps across the last of the water and up the low embankment.

The grey packhorse, always the sure-footed one, followed close behind. Once on the dry land, Eli stepped down and allowed both horses to shake off the excess and looked about for a spot for a midday camp and room for a small fire to brew some coffee.

# CHAPTER 17

## MOUNTAINS

As he swung aboard Rusty, Eli stood in the stirrups and lifted his eyes to the west and spotted a line of green that fell from the higher mountains. Shading his eyes from the early afternoon sun that hung high in the brassy sky, he saw the far blue mountains to the west and north. He let a slow grin split his face as he dropped back into the seat of his saddle, reached down to stroke Rusty's neck, "Well boy, let's head west by north. The mountains yonder are callin' us!" and nudged Rusty to the trail.

It was an old but well-used trail, he spotted a few cairns that showed age as they stood just off the trail, some with grey sticks, arrow shafts, and branches used by passersby of ancient times to indicate the route of travel taken, probably by others of the same village. Although a narrow trail, it showed sign of the passing of travois that carried lodges and more. A slight breeze stirred off his left shoulder, the cool air coming down from the mountains, and he turned to look at the vast plain of grass that moved like the waves of the sea.

Anytime he thought of the sea, his mind traveled into the past and the days of his youth and the ways of his stern father, Homer, who sought to make him a ship-builder after the family tradition. The McCain Ship-builders of Essex built some of the finest schooners, and his father was proud of the heritage and hoped Elijah would take the same pride and continue the legacy. Eli had worked throughout the shop from scarfing on the keel, as a dubber on the futtocks, caulking with oakum and the iron and mallet, with the joiners to build the hatches and galley, and even with the carvers on the figurehead. When the smells, heat, and sweat of the hard woodwork inside became unbearable, he worked outside with the sparmakers and riggers.

He learned much, but what he learned best was that he did not want to be a shipbuilder. His father insisted he take a least one turn as a deckhand on one of their schooners and after a year at sea, doing everything possible aboard the ship, the best lessons learned were in the ports when he had more than his share of rough-and-tumble fighting, but he came out more the man than before. When the ship finally hove to at the home port of Essex, he found his land legs and a renewed determina-tion to stay as far away from saltwater as he could. Because of his father's connections with politicians and bureaucrats in the government, he managed to get an appointment to West Point and after graduation he headed west, his back to the sea and his eyes to the mountains.

The trail he traveled rode the rolling hills, keeping the little willow-lined creek off his left shoulder. A glance to his right showed a long, low flattop mesa that tapered off to the east, its steep sides showing the same grasses as the flats. The trail split the flats between the mesa and the creek that came from a deeper canyon that cut through the timber-topped foothills. The hills between him and the creek showed rocky shoulders among the piñon and cedar, and the trail took him over a bench that revealed the rocky canyon on his left and a narrow valley to his right that promised water where the trail bent to the north and split two rocky-topped buttes.

As he dropped from the bench, he heard the chuckles and giggles of a little stream that cascaded from the high mountains and made a loop around a small knob that lay between the two rocky buttes. A glance to the sky showed he had another couple hours of daylight and he determined to water the horses and himself, and push on up the valley before making camp. He was anxious to get into the timbered mountains where he felt more at home.

As he approached the chuckling stream, Eli reined up and stepped down, looking around carefully but unobtrusively, paying close attention to the skirt of thick timber that covered the east face of the round-topped butte on his left. The horses took their drink, stepped back, and had their own look-see, but neither showed concern and watched as Eli went to one knee and scooped up water in one hand for his quick drink from the Little Pipestone Creek. He stepped back beside Rusty, looked at the rocky knob and what appeared to be a bench at a slight break in the timber that invited him to the crest for a better look. He swung aboard Rusty and turned back to take the lesser trail that crossed the bench and crested the rise behind the butte. Once there, he stopped, grabbed the binoculars from the saddlebags, and with the horses ground tied on some grass, he walked to the top of the butte and bellied down for a good long survey of the valley below.

Directly north, the low foothills held a plateau dimpled with piñon and juniper, with nothing promising in the distance but more terrain much the same. The main trail he was following sided the creek in the bottom that came from the west and appeared to cut through the timbered hills and swing from the north. Many of the south-facing slopes of the hills were bald, but the north-facing slopes were black with timber. Southwest of him a big mountain held court with the lesser hills, its hoary head of granite still showing snow in the clefts and ravines that aged the old mountain. But it was the lesser hills, still black with timber, that invited Eli to make his way through, the trail traveled by the ancients pointing the way.

As he scanned the hills, the only movement he saw was a nearby coyote digging after a reclusive rabbit and a big buck still in the velvet tiptoeing to the water further upstream. He watched the mule deer, looked around and seeing nothing else moving, he rose from his promontory and returned to the horses. He had spotted a likely place for a camp up a slight draw off the creek below. If it held true to its promise, it would be a comfortable and secure camp for the night.

To many, the narrow trail through the tall timber would feel confining with towering spruce and fir trees scratching the heavens, but to Eli it was a comforting place with its pungent smell of pines, the whisper of the wind through the trees, the treetops waving to and fro as if offering a welcoming invitation to venture further. Two cow elk, trailing new orange calves, pushed through the trees below him, stopping to investigate the intruder, then moving on, unconcerned. Two red squirrels raced one another up a tall spruce, stopped and looked at Eli, and scolded him in their ceaseless chatter as he rode past.

The spruce, fir, and pines parted for a shank of aspen that climbed the draw toward the higher mountains, quaking their leaves to flirt with the rider and his two horses, and offering a brief glimpse of blue sky before the trail ducked back into the dark forest. The air around the aspen gave a different scent, powdery and dry but pleasant, the leaves of previous falls layered upon the ground quieting the hooves of the horses. As he pushed into the woods, the only sounds were the creak of leather from his saddle, the occasional clatter of hooves on a rock, but mostly the carpet of pine needles offered a silent passing.

The trail dipped across a low arroyo, rose over the low and almost bald shoulder of a foothill, and dropped into the coulee sighted by Eli from his promontory almost two miles back down the draw. He paused at the edge of the trees, looking at the willows that sided the little creek before it joined the slightly bigger creek in the valley followed by the trail. He stood in his stirrups, looking up the draw and across the coulee to the partially bald shoulder of the next hill. Seeing nothing, he nudged Rusty forward, but the stallion did not move. His head was turned up the coulee, his eyes wide and nostrils flaring, ears pointing. Something was bothering him. Eli twisted in the saddle to look at the grey, saw he was acting much the same and both animals twitched, nervousness moving their hooves as they sidestepped, alarmed. Eli leaned down, stroked the stallion's neck, "Easy boy, easy now."

The creek in the bottom was thick with willows, alders, and tall aspen. The little feeder creek was hidden by willows, kinnikinnick, and chokecherry. A break in the pines at the edge of the valley offered the best site for a camp. There was deadfall for firewood, grass for the animals, and tall trees for shelter. Although the woods were sprinkled with the dead snags standing like grey skeletons and crackling and groaning in the breeze, most of the trees were tall and green and it was a pleasant place. Eli stepped down, led the timid horses from the trees to the clearing, and began to strip them before rubbing them down. He chuckled as they both did a good roll in the dirt, stood, shook their heads and rolled their hides, then looked at Eli and down to the creek and followed as he led them to the water.

He stroked Rusty's neck, "So, whatever had you spooked is gone, is it?" looking about and watching both horses as he stood beside them. When they finished their drink, he walked them back to the clearing, picketed them, but did not tie them fast. Not knowing what had spooked them earlier, he wanted them to be able to free themselves if necessary, and he knew they knew when they were tethered tight or not. They dropped their heads to the grass and Eli went to the packs and began making his camp. First was the coffeepot, and he soon had the little fire going and water heating.

Eli had lain his bedroll out between two grey logs, two big firs that had left the grey trunks as the last vestige of their presence, but now would provide good protection for Eli. He sat on one, finishing the last of his coffee and jerky which was his only supper for this night, and sat watching the last of the coals glimmer under the ashes, and glanced to the remaining gold-bottomed clouds that lingered in the sky. A few stars had already lighted their lanterns, and the moon was hinting at its presence with a glimmer of light in the east. Darkness was stretching its black fingers through the branches of the shadowy trees and layering its quiet on the willows and aspen. The horses stood hipshot near the big ponderosa as Eli dropped into his blankets. He lay with his hands clasped behind his head as he watched the stars shed their shyness and thought of his journey and his hopefulness at finding the boys. He closed his eyes and muttered his prayers for the night, rolled over and tucked his hands under his cheek, eyes closing in anticipation of sleep, when the scream, taunts, and barks of a mountain lion split the stillness and rocked the tops of the trees.

Eli sat up, the big Spencer rifle in his hands as he eared back the hammer, looking about. A quick glance to the horses saw them with heads high, ears pricked, nostrils flaring as they sidestepped and blew. Rusty looked at Eli and Eli searched the trees, standing slowly, looking about. The scream seemed to come from all around them, telling Eli the cougar was on the hunt and near. The huffing and coughing at the end of its scream wafted through the trees, as Eli unconsciously backed closer to the horses.

A sudden flash of pale fur launched itself from a big branch on a massive spruce, the branch bouncing when the weight left, but the big cougar, feet and claws outstretched, mouth wide and teeth bared, targeted the grey packhorse. The beast landed on the back of the horse, claws digging into its shoulders and its teeth buried at the base of its neck. The grey bucked, squealed, kicked, and tore free of its tether, charging into the trees. The big stallion had swapped ends and kicked at the beast as the grey ran past. Eli lifted the Spencer, trying for a shot, but the pounce happened so quickly in the dark and the running horse had charged past, and Eli was unable to get a shot.

He ran to the stallion, grabbed the lead and ripped it

free, swung aboard the horse and dug heels into his ribs to give chase. The big horse leaped, stretched out, and charged into the trees, letting the lances of pale light from the big moon show the trail before them. The battle for life was happening before them and the grey had carried the cougar no more than thirty yards down the trail. Eli saw the animals, the grey bucking and kicking, turning his head around and biting at the cougar, both fighting for life. Eli dropped to the ground, dropped to one knee, and brought the big Spencer to his shoulder, searching for an instant of a shot. The grey dove under a low branch trying to scrape off the cougar, but the claws were deep and held. The grey stumbled, reared up and dropped his head between his front hooves, kicked high with his heels and crow-hopped near a dead snag, turned and fell against the towering trunk, smashing the body of the cougar between his weight and the standing trunk.

He scampered to his feet, the cougar hanging on with one paw, and Eli fired. The bullet tore into the chest of the cougar, prompting a snarl and cough, but another bullet tore into the cougar's shoulder, dropping him from the back of the grey. The beast twisted and squirmed on the ground, trying to right itself, but the forest was blasted with another roar from the Spencer as the killing slug bore into the skull of the beast, driving it to the ground to lie still in death.

The grey was stumbling about, head hanging, chest heaving, and Eli walked toward him, hand out, speaking softly, "Easy, boy, easy." As he neared, he saw the deep claw marks from the beast, blood trailing from the wounds of the claws and those at the base of his neck from the cougar's fangs. The little grey was hurt and hurt bad. He looked at Eli with frightened and sad eyes as Eli stood beside his neck, his arm over the mane and stroking the far side as his left hand held the Spencer at his side. Eli looked down at the horse, who turned to look up at Eli, and knew he had to doctor this animal and not put him down. If it was possible to help him heal, he had to do it. This faithful horse had been with him since his last years at Fort Laramie and through much of the war. Although it seemed like a long time, it was only five years, which made the little grey about seven, eight years old and that wasn't old for a horse. The man and his two horses walked back to the camp, Eli between the two, all moving slowly, patient with the stumbling grey, wondering about the coming days.

# CHAPTER 18

## DOCTORIN'

E ver the student of the wilderness and the ways of the natives, Eli had learned from all the tribes he had been with during his time at Fort Laramie. He knew the grey needed the wounds cleaned, and a poultice applied to each of the wounds. He had some Balm of Gilead made from the buds of aspen trees in his packs, but he wanted to save that for himself if possible or would use it later. Other things could be done now. After returning to the camp, he did what he could in the dim light of the moon, made a quick trip through the willows and grasses near the creek, searching for the Bee Balm plant and the Fireweed, both common to this type of country and at this time of year. But the search for the plants would have to wait for morning's light, so he fetched water for the initial washing of the wounds.

As the sun still hid beyond the eastern horizon, the dim light of early morning gave Eli sufficient light to begin his gathering. The long stems and purple flower gave away the Bee Balm and he gathered a hat full of the leaves. The tall stem with the tiny pink flowers told of the Fireweed. He grabbed a couple of stems and jerked them from the soil, knocking off the dirt and breaking off the stem. The roots would be used with the leaves of the Bee Balm as the beginning of the poultice. He stacked his gathering at the bottom of the slope, turned away, and started toward the far hillside for some sage. With his hat full of sage leaves, he returned to his trove and carried his bounty back to camp. He put them all in the Dutch oven to which he added water to cover them and hung the pot over the fire.

He used the water in his canteen to begin washing the wounds on the grey who hung his head, often trembling, as Eli gently tended the wounds. He carefully looked at the deepest wounds, those made by the front claws, and knew some of those would need to be stitched together for them to heal properly. As he washed, the clotted blood gave way and the wounds bled, but that is what was needed for the fresh blood to help in cleaning the wounds, but he made quick work of the washing and returned to the pot. The water had heated through and was bubbling to a boil when Eli removed it from the fire, scooping out the leaves and roots to lay on the rock. He used the water to do some additional cleansing of the wounds, knowing the added strength of the leaves and roots would be an antiseptic.

Grey seemed to appreciate the ministering, lifting his head and turning sad eyes to Eli, but he did not resist, although the trembles occasionally returned, but the warm water seemed to comfort him. He used the big rock and another smooth stone to pound the leaves and the roots into a poultice. He had gathered some big pads of a prickly pear and gave them a quick run through the flames to burn off the spines and little needles. When he could handle the pads, he sliced them open, used the green gelatinous inside to hold the poultice and applied the pads and poultices to each of the wounds. With the fresh hide of a young buck, he made a bandage, wrapping the lengths of the hide over Grey's neck and under each leg and back again. It was a sight to see, but it looked like it was going to hold.

Surprisingly, the few wounds to his hindquarters were not as deep and fewer in number. Eli wondered if the lion had been injured or if something kept him from doing what most lions were known to do and use his hind legs to practically gut their quarry. But the wounds, once washed and dabbed with the poultice makings, were left to the open air to aid healing. Satisfied he had done all he could for now, he decided to cut some of the tall grasses and bring it Grey so he would not have to move around to eat. He also used the big pot to fetch some water for him to drink. As he sat the pot before the grey, the gelding looked at him, looked over at Rusty who stood watching the goings-on, and dipped his nose in the water for a long drink.

Eli walked to Rusty, put his arm over his neck and leaned close, "Well, boy, looks like we're gonna be takin' care of your buddy here for a while. Leastways until he can get around better. There's too much for you to carry since you're packin' me and the rest of the gear, so we'll just rest up a mite and let ol' grey get better, what say?" He chuckled as he stroked Rusty's neck and behind his ears. But Rusty lifted his head, looking back down the long draw that held the trail and the creek. His ears were pricked, and his nostrils flared, but it was not the kind of fear shown before with the lion.

Where Eli had traveled the lesser trail that wound through the woods, the main trail sided the creek in the bottom and was out in the open. This was the trail used by most travelers that came this way and now the sounds of hooves clattering on hard-packed dirt and rocks told of riders approaching. Eli stood still, watching through the trees, knowing the lack of sounds of saddle leather creaking or shod hooves clattering on rocks, said these were Natives.

Eli stepped away from the horses and retrieved his Winchester, stood behind the trunk of a big ponderosa, and watched as the travelers neared. Six riders came into view, four men and two women, Blackfeet. Eli recognized them as Piikani, as the men often wore their hair loose, but with a topknot that held one or more feathers. The man in the lead looked familiar and Eli recognized Running Rabbit with his woman Prairie Flower and behind them rode the very familiar Morning Dove. The other warriors looked familiar, but he could not name them. As they neared, Eli stepped from behind the tree and stood with his rifle cradled in his left arm, his right hand lifted high, and he called, *"Okii Nikso' kowaiksi!"* Which was to say, Hello my friends! He grinned as they stopped and stared, but the sun was at Eli's back and they shaded their eyes. He watched Running Rabbit slowly smile and nudge his mount forward. He spoke over his shoulder to the others, *"Nikso'sowaiksi,* Eli." The others followed, but Morning Dove pushed her mount forward alongside Running Rabbit and quickly dropped to the ground. She ran up to Eli and embraced him, "Eli! You make me happy to see you. I have looked for you often." She stepped to his side, slipped her hand through his crooked arm, and pulled herself close as she looked at Running Rabbit and Prairie Flower with an embarrassed grin, then dropped her eyes to the ground. It was not the way of the Blackfeet people to be so expressive with their emotions, especially with one who was not of their people.

"Welcome to my camp. Step down, we will share a meal."

The chief looked at his woman, glanced to the others, and with a slight nod stepped to the ground and greeted Eli as they grasped forearms. As they walked the short distance into Eli's camp, the chief told of moving their village from north of the Boulder River south to the Big Pipestone Creek, but their names for the river and creeks given in the tongue of the Piikani. The village would be their summer encampment in an area that had not been hunted for several seasons and promised an unusual abundance of game. "We are here to get the red pipestone to make pipes for our people. It is a good stone, easy to carve and does not break with the heat of the tobacco." They entered the little clearing where Eli's horses were picketed, both looking up at the visitors and Rusty nickering as he recognized the scent of mares nearing their season. With his nostrils flared, head held high, he pranced side to side, straining at his tether, as the horses neared. The people also recognized the actions of both the mares and Rusty, smiles crossed the faces of all as they watched. Prairie Flower asked her man, "Where do we put our mares?"

Running Rabbit looked to Eli with eyebrows raised and a grin splitting his face as if asking permission to let Rusty breed the mares. Eli chuckled, "We can take them down near the creek. The grass is tall, and they won't go far."

Running Rabbit motioned to the other warriors to tether their animals and take the two mares of the women to follow Eli and Rusty to the grassy flat beside the small creek. The animals had no sooner been loosed, than the courtship began with both mares competing for attention from the big claybank stallion.

While the men tended the animals, the women had quickly surveyed the camp and began the preparation of the morning meal. Eli and Running Rabbit went to the side of the grey and Eli told of the fight with the cougar. The chief tenderly stroked the grey, looking at the bandages and felt the tension and nervousness of the gelding. "Most would let the animal go, help it to cross over and end the pain, but you have tended this one like a friend. Why?"

"We," nodding to the grey, "have been through much together. He was a wild horse I took near Fort Laramie and has been a faithful friend. We went through much of the white man's war together, and I have to do what I can. If he does not heal, then I'll put him down."

The chief nodded his understanding as they turned back to the camp, sat opposite one another, Eli on the edge of the big flat rock, his back to the fire, Running Rabbit on the grey log. The chief asked, "Your search for your sons?"

"Haven't found them yet, but I'm going to Bear Gulch, a new gold find, and I'm hopeful I might find some sign of the boys."

"If you do not?"

"Dunno, but I cannot give up. My word was given to my dying wife, and I cannot fail."

"It is good what you do. If you find them and they do not want to return?"

"Well, since my wife has crossed over, it must be the decision of my sons as to what they will do."

Morning Dove and Prairie Flower had heard the men as they discussed the grey horse and the cougar, and

Morning Dove came to Eli's side, "Would you like for me to help with the healing of your horse?"

Eli grinned, nodding, "He will need his bandages and poultices changed after midday, if you are here, I would like that."

Morning Dove nodded, smiling, and turned away to resume her duties at the fire with Prairie Flower.

The chief chuckled, looked at Eli, "Since you left our village, she has been long faced. When our warriors return from a hunt or anytime the sound of horses coming into the village, she runs to see if it is you. You must do something."

Eli slowly shook his head, "What do you think I should do? I must do what I can to keep my word to my wife."

"But she would be helpful in your search and your nights would be warm, if she is with you." The chief grinned and chuckled mischievously and knowingly. "She is the sister of my woman and helps her, but..." he chuckled again, glancing from Eli to the fire and back.

# CHAPTER 19

## COMPANY

"I will stay with Eli until you return," explained Morning Dove as she sat beside Prairie Flower on the big log. The breakfast had been finished and the other warriors had chosen to go afoot up the small arroyo in search of game; the chief, his woman, and Morning Dove staying behind, listening and watching the antics of the romantic trio of horses below the camp. "I will help him tend to his injured horse and you will come back to this camp after you have the pipestone." She had made her decision without talking to Eli, declaring her intentions to both her sister and her husband, Running Rabbit.

The chief grinned as he glanced to his woman and Eli. Eli shrugged in acceptance, thinking their excursion for the pipestone would be brief and they would return before the day was over. He said, "We will talk when you return." The grin on Running Rabbit's face and that of his woman, hinted that it might be a few days and nights before they returned.

Eli had been attracted to Morning Dove the first

time they met when he had helped the chief back to his camp after their short fight with the Lakota. She had been charged with tending to the needs of their new friend and the two spent most of the time together, both attracted to one another and at his parting, she had promised to wait for him until he had fulfilled the covenant made with his dying wife. The fires of attraction that had been kindled on their first time together had not waned and they both wanted to be together, but Eli's commitment to what he knew was right would not allow him to be with a woman that was not his wife.

Among the people of the Piikani, the lines of what was not allowed and what was practiced were not as pronounced nor definite. But Eli fought with himself and his commitments as he considered taking Morning Dove as his mate or wife. His concern was not for what others might think or judge, caring little for the acceptance of others, but only for his own standards and morals but also to honor the ways and teachings of his Lord. As he pictured the two of them together, with her at his side and being a friend, companion, and helper, he smiled at the thought of what it would be like to have her beside him, knowing it would be pleasing and even fulfilling. He sighed heavily as he turned his gaze from the fire to the face of his friend, who had been watching Eli make the journey through his mind and memories, knowing the thoughts of a man as he considered taking a woman as his wife.

Running Rabbit lowered his voice, glanced at the women as they did the cleanup after the meal, and said, "If you choose and want, we could have the joining ceremony here when we return from the pipestone place." He grinned and chuckled as he watched the expression on Eli's face turn from reflection and contemplation to surprise and even fear.

The chief stood, spoke to the women, "We must go, the day will soon shed its light and we have not taken any stone." He nodded to the low end of the camp, "Our warriors return. We must get the mares and make ready."

———

ELI AND MORNING Dove stood together as they watched the party of Running Rabbit and Prairie Flower ride from their camp and turn up the trail toward the headwaters of the Little Pipestone Creek. Morning Dove turned to Eli with a smile, "I will check the bandages of the grey horse and then gather more plants to make more."

Eli nodded as they turned back to the camp, "That will be good. I had not planned to stay here, but Grey must be tended and heal before we will travel more. I will get Rusty and your mare and bring them back into the camp."

"It is good," replied Morning Dove. The conversation was a little awkward, but they both were glad to be alone together. There was much to talk about and decide about besides tending to horses, but about the days ahead.

Eli paused as Morning Dove continued into the camp, watched her walk away and shook his head as a slow grin painted his face. He turned away and started for the bottom of the draw where the mare and stallion had been romping. He saw the two horses nuzzling one another, showing no interest in grazing nor taking water, just staying close together, never losing touch with one another. Eli shook his head at the thought of how the horses were no different than he and Morning Dove, but they were not bound by tradition, beliefs, nor commitments, just the enjoyment of the moment.

Morning Dove's horse was a dark palomino with flaxen mane and tail, a star on her forehead and stood about fifteen and a half hands. Well-built with a big rump, broad chest, short back, and soft eyes, the temperament of the horse showed in the way she shouldered the bigger stallion around, never nipping, but often nickering and accepting of the stallion's attentions. They made a good pair, their coloring complimenting one another with the red lineback marking of the stallion, the coloring that was spoken of as a claybank resembling the coloring of the red clay in the bank of the creeks similar to that where the people of Running Rabbit obtained their pipestone. The stallion stood a good sixteen hands and had a well-muscled body and long legs that was common to the Tennessee Walker breed, and the muscular build telling of the Morgan breed. The blaze face and three stockings accented the coloring and gave a bit of flash to the look of the stallion.

Eli walked to the horses and noticed how Rusty was protective of the mare, even standing between Eli and the mare, his stance showing ownership. Eli grinned, spoke to his mount, "Now, Rusty, I'm not here to ruin your time together." He reached out, catching hold of the halter and stroking the face of the stallion, rubbing behind his ears as the stallion lowered his head and pushed against Eli's chest with his nose. The mare came close beside, and Eli reached for her halter, turned, and led the two animals up the slight rise to the camp. He picketed them together away from the grey and walked back to the fire where Morning Dove was tending a mix in the Dutch oven that hung over the little fire.

She smiled at Eli, "I picked some plants and will make another poultice for the grey horse. His wounds were deep, but they are looking good, you sewed them well. It will take some time to heal."

"That's what I figgered, a couple days at least."

"You did well with your poultices and bandages. He," nodding to the packhorse, is calm now. He drank much and was eating some. That is good." She paused, looked at Eli, "The cougar, where is the hide?"

Eli chuckled, "Still on him. I was too concerned about the horses to worry about the cat."

"Where is it? The hide makes a soft leather, and I will do that for you," she smiled.

Eli pointed to the break in the trees and the ancient trail that led to the carcass, "A short ways down that trail. But the smell of that hide will spook the horses."

"Yes, but if I get the hide, I will take it to the stream to begin the work. When I am finished, there will be no scent of the cougar."

————

MORNING DOVE TENDED to her preparations for the poultices, changed the bandages on the grey, and left the camp to skin out the cougar. Eli had gathered his weapons and began the cleaning, oiling, and more that had been delayed far too long. It gave him time to reflect and consider his future and the possibility of joining with Morning Dove. His mind chased memories and possibilities and dreams while his hands worked busily at the task before him.

Morning Dove had skinned out the cat, deboned the better cuts of meat from the carcass and taken the hide to the grasses beside the smaller creek, and with a quick look at the hide, a bit of initial scraping to strip the worst of the membrane and meat, she put the hide in the water, weighted it down with rocks, and washed her hands and arms to rid them of the scent and returned to the camp. The broad smile of Eli gave Morning Dove a warm feeling that swept over her and her smile reflected that of Eli's as she neared the one she considered to be her man. She sat beside him, quietly watching as he finished cleaning the Colt revolver shotgun, the last of his weapons to be cleaned. When he finished, he reassembled the shotgun and lay it aside with the other weapons. She smiled at him, and asked, "Would you like some coffee?"

"Yes, thank you," he answered, watching her move away and drop to her heels to pick up the coffeepot and pour him a fresh cup. He smiled at her graceful movements, her pleasant smile and the look in her eyes that told of affection if not love, but when she returned to give him the cup and sat down beside him, her hand resting on his knee, the warmth of her presence was pleasing. *Maybe this is a good thing.*

# CHAPTER 20

## COMMITMENT

The rattle of trace chains, the rumble of wagon wheels on the hard-packed trail, and the clatter of horse hooves brought Eli instantly awake. He rolled from his blankets, rifle in hand, jacking a round into the chamber and searching the trees between his camp and the trail for whatever was causing the ruckus as the first grey light showed in the east. The shouts of men and the thunderous commotion told of the presence of white men, probably gold hunters that were oblivious to the need for quiet when traveling through Indian country. Eli stepped to the trees, using the tall ponderosa for cover, and looked below and beyond the creek bottom to the roadway used by the prospectors and settlers as their route to the goldfields. One wagon with a four-up team, led by two riders and followed by four others, was making the beginning of the long climb into the mountains. Dust rose from the wagon wheels, almost obscuring the trailing riders, while the lead riders were trotting their mounts, one man standing in his stirrups to see further up the road, wondering what lay before them, the other man twisting around in his saddle to check their back trail, at least what he could see through the dust cloud.

The driver was cracking his bull whip over the heads of the team, hollering his threats and curses all the while, and the squeal of a dry hub told of the impending breakdown. But the squeal rose, the hub and spindle screeched, and the wheel slid in the dirt, bringing the wagon to a stop as it slid to the side of the trail. One of the leaders shouted, "What's wrong back there?"

"It's that wheel! We gotta grease it, maybe change it!" shouted the driver, as the dust cloud billowed around him and he sought vainly to wave it away.

The driver tied off the lines to the break lever, stepped on the wheel and the hub, and dropped to the ground to examine the hub of the back wheel that was smoking. He looked up and hollered to the leader, "It might be froze up! I need some help here!"

The leader turned his horse back to the wagon, dropped to the ground with a glance to the driver and the wheel, and looked to the trailing riders that now sat leaning on their pommels, "You four, get down here an help Pops with this wheel!"

"Why don't we leave it! Them Sioux are not too far behind us and if they catch up..."

"We need the tools and supplies in that wagon more'n we need you, Skeeter, so get down here and help so we can get it fixed 'fore them Injuns catch up!" ordered the leader, a big barrel-chested man that stood well over six feet and probably topped the scales near three hundred pounds. His size was not the convincing part of the argument, it was the cocked Remington pistol in his hand.

Morning Dove came to Eli's side, "Who are they?" she whispered.

"Gold hunters, but I heard 'em say there were some Sioux followin' 'em."

Morning Dove frowned, "The Sioux would not be following unless they did something, maybe they had a fight or something and the Sioux want vengeance."

"That's kinda what I was thinkin'. The one man said the wagon had tools and supplies, so they're gold hunters alright, but..." he shrugged as he watched the goings-on of the bunch. From Eli's camp to the road was about a hundred yards, but the steep walls of the canyon and the morning air easily carried any and all sounds so that Eli could hear and understand most of what was said. As the men worked, they grumbled and complained, but the big man who appeared to be their leader had mounted up and rode further up the road, scouting the trail before them.

Two of the men were leaning on the long skinny bit of a tree they used to lift the wagon by the lever they devised, with a big rock two men rolled behind the wagon. Another man was rolling the spare wheel toward the hub and the fourth man was greasing the spindle. The two with the lever were the most verbal of the complainers and one grumbled to his partner, "I'd like to drop this wagon on him," nodding toward the leader as he rode away.

"Don't let him hear you say that!" answered the second man.

"I didn't join this bunch to be bossed around by him. He ain't no different or better'n the rest of us. What gives him the right to bark orders at us?"

The second man shook his head, "You wanna argue

with him, go right ahead, just make sure I ain't no where around."

"Hey Pops!" hollered one of the lever holders, looking at the two by the wheel, "How far back you think them Injuns are?"

The older man called Pops showed a touch of grey hair around his friar ring that separated his bald pate from his ears. He had dropped his hat when he started greasing the spindle, and grumbled his answer, "Oh, mebbe a couple hours, dependin'..."

"Dependin'? Dependin' on what?"

"How mad they are at Baker an' what he done with that squaw woman. I reckon they's purty mad since they been on our tail fer a day an' a half. That squaw musta belonged to somebody important, mebbe a war leader or sumpin'." He grumbled as he scooted back away from the spindle to help the other man with the wheel. "Now, quit yammerin' and lift this wagon!" ordered Pops, as he and the other man scooted the wheel near the spindle. As they watched the wagon lift, they lifted the wheel onto the spindle and the older man grabbed up the wagon nut and began spinning it on the spindle of the axle. He grabbed up the wrench and tightened the nut, nodded to the men, and they lowered the wagon to put the weight on the axle and wheels.

"Hey! Get a move on! We're wastin' time!" came the shout from the leader who had returned from his scout up the trail. He watched as the grumbling men went to their horses and Pops climbed up on the wagon. With a shout and a crack of the whip, the horses leaned into their traces and the wagon moved without a squeal of the wheels and the group resumed their journey up the trail beside the Little Pipestone Creek.

As Eli turned toward the camp, Morning Dove asked, "If those men see my people, they will fight!"

"Ummhmm, and if they run into the Sioux, there's gonna be a fight." He looked at Morning Dove. "You know this country and where your people will be, is it possible we could get to them before they do and warn them about both the white men and the Sioux?"

Morning Dove frowned, thinking about where they were and where her people had gone to get the pipestone. It had been a few years since she was here last, and she struggled to remember. She looked at Eli, "I believe to where my people are, the creek turns back into the mountains, away from this road. It is one hand of time to where it leaves the road."

Eli frowned, glancing to the sky, knowing when she said one hand, it was the same as four fingers of the sun's movement. When looking at the sun and the horizon, the movement of the sun is about a quarter hour for every finger that is held at arm's length with the hand flat and on edge, palm toward your face. The breadth of a finger is the measurement and four fingers, or one hand, is about an hour of time.

"That is not enough time to overtake them and get to your people before they do," surmised Eli, frowning.

"My people will not be seen by such as those," stated Morning Dove, referring to the noisy white men. "They will be heard long before my people come from the pipestone."

"But what about the Sioux? If they're following that bunch and are on the prod, won't they fight your people?"

"Was it not a fight with the Sioux that brought you to our camp when we first met? You brought our chief,

Running Rabbit, to our village after your fight, is that not so?" asked Morning Dove.

"Yeah, it was a fight with the Sioux," he paused, "So, if your people run into the bunch that's after those men, there will be a fight?"

"Yes."

"Then we better make ready. We'll leave the grey here at camp, but I'll need to take all my weapons, and we'll wait to see how many Sioux there are and if they're really following that bunch. That way, we can follow them and if they have a run-in with your people, we'll be behind them and help."

Morning Dove grinned and leaned her head against Eli's shoulder, "It is good that we fight our enemy together. I am a warrior of my people, and you are a great warrior. We will take many scalps of the Sioux!"

Eli turned to look directly at Morning Dove with his eyebrows lifted in a questioning expression, "I don't take scalps," he proclaimed, shaking his head as he looked at this woman in a different light, trying to picture this beautiful woman that exuded nothing but femininity as a screaming warrior ripping off the scalp of an enemy. He shook his head at the thought, sighed heavily, relieved that he was not her enemy.

# CHAPTER 21

## SKIRMISH

Eli reached for the saddle horn as he lifted his foot to the stirrup, but Rusty suddenly lifted his head, ears pricked, sidestepped, as he bent his head around to look toward the creek bottom. Eli glanced to Morning Dove's mare to see she too was skittish. Eli moved to the trees for a look below and spotted riders coming, the war party of Sioux that looked to be about fifteen strong. The clatter of hooves from up the road showed two more riders, probably scouts, returning to the war party. As they pulled up, the scouts and leaders talked, scouts excitedly motioning up the road. The war leader turned to talk to the rest of the war party, relaying the news from the scouts and excitement spread through the ranks of the warriors as they stifled war cries and more. War lances were shaken overhead, buffalo hide shields were lifted, bows waved high, as the war leader gave his orders.

The warriors split into two groups, one group following one of the scouts and taking to the higher trail that moved through the thick pines on the same side of the creek where Eli's camp lay, the other staying on the roadway. They moved out at a rapid pace, yet for so many warriors, the noise was at a minimum. Eli turned to Morning Dove. "They'll be goin' for the white men. If Running Rabbit and his people are wary, this bunch should pass them by, depending on how fast the white men are moving. But if they're already on the road coming back..." he shrugged.

"Do we follow?" asked Morning Dove, a mix of anger and fear turning to determination as she watched the Sioux move away.

"Yeah, but we'll follow that bunch," nodding toward the band that took to the trail that cut through the trees.

———

THE ROADWAY WAS LITTLE MORE than two ruts that hugged the north slope of thickly timbered hillside. The road sided the Little Pipestone Creek that was obscured by willows and alders with tall grasses abundant among the brush. The black timber was speckled with dead snags that stood as grey skeletons as reminders from some long-ago severe winter that killed off many of the fir and spruce that refused to give way to the new growth timber that covered the mountain slopes. Green leafed aspen quaked among the pines, usually preferring the moister bottoms of ravines and draws, with their pale green leaves offering accents to the darker greens that showed almost black as they painted the steep hillsides.

The narrow road bent to the north, following the carved-out arroyo of the little creek but always pointing the way to the new goldfields. The heavy-loaded wagon rumbled, lifting dust to coat the tarpaulin that covered the cargo and hung in the air to stifle the four riders that followed. It was nearing midday and the men had been traveling all morning without a stop when a side draw appeared with an ancient trail that followed the creek as it crossed the road and chuckled from the north. Baker lifted his hand to stop the wagon and the other men, "We'll pull off there, give the horses a break, and have some coffee and such. I think we're far enough ahead o' them Injuns that we can take a few."

The other riders welcomed the break, but Skeeter, always the one to complain, "Why can't we fix us somethin' to eat instead o' that jerky stuff?"

"You're welcome to fix any kinda meal you want, Skeeter, but the rest of us will be long gone while you're stuffin' yore face an' sharin' your food with the Injuns!" growled Baker, shaking his head as he stepped down from his mount, loosened the girth, and led the horse to the little creek. The creek was no more than two feet across and less than a hand breadth deep, but it was cool, clear, and inviting. The other men joined Baker at the water, spacing out along the bank and letting their horses drink first, all except Skeeter.

Pops was busy with the team, stripping off as much of the harness as necessary to give them the freedom to get a good drink and some graze. Riley and Pence gathered some firewood while Bugs and Whitey readied the fire and the coffee. Everyone had brought their coffee cups and grabbed a handful of jerky from the bag in the wagon. Riley, the Irishman with red hair and freckles, was the youngest of the group while Pence was a blonde-haired, square-built German and was the next oldest to Pops. Bugs had eyes that bugged out from his narrow hatchet face that gave him his nickname, and Whitey was probably approaching the low side of thirty and prided himself in his appearance, with boots that always showed a shine, except when covered with road dust, and preferred anything black. The slash of white hair that painted the left side of his head above his ears from his forehead to the back of his head accented the raven black hair. Pops had white hair, what there was of it in a friar ring above his ears, a skeletal frame but eyes that pierced through the doubt and fear of others. Baker, the self-appointed leader, was the biggest and probably the meanest of the bunch and used his size to bully anyone that got in his way and had never been beaten in any fight, whether rough-and-tumble or shootout.

They were an odd bunch, looking more like a gang of thieves than partners searching for gold, but they had come together on the journey from the east and now were determined to see it through until they all had their pokes full of gold. Single-minded after hearing tales of rich strikes, the ne'er-do-wells had fanciful dreams of riches, thinking only of the gold and never giving a thought to the dangers of the wilderness and the tribes whose homeland they invaded. But now they were all fearful of the Sioux that were on their trail because two nights past when they camped near a river and unknown to them, a village of the Sioux, Baker had found a woman getting water and had his way with her, leaving her dead body in the bushes to be found by the men of the Sioux encampment.

Baker swore he did nothing wrong, declaring every woman fought a little, but they had to be taught what a man wanted. The others had looked at one another and needed no further explanation, they had seen Baker around women and had to deal with his ways before. He had been a master sergeant in the Union Army and had a reputation of barking orders and if they were not imme-diately obeyed, he forced his way with his size and his authority, commonly bullying the troops into submission to his will.

He walked among the men as if he was still in the army, demanding their obedience, but only one of the men had been in the army, the others were runaways from conscription or layabouts that had no interest in the war. Baker snarled at the others as they fixed their coffee and scrounged among the crates and boxes for jerky and other foodstuffs. Whitey flipped up the lid of the coffeepot and dropped a handful of grounds into the water, slid the pot back toward the flames, and sat back to chew on his jerky as he watched the pot begin to dance.

Bugs jumped to his feet, pointing toward the trees, stammering and stuttering, his eyes bigger than usual, but nonsensical gibberish fell from his lips as he did a dance. Riley said, "What? You ain't makin' no sense, Bugs!" looking in the direction of his pointing. He looked around, searching for his rifle as an arrow whispered past the wagon, impaling itself in Riley's neck, making his eyes bug out like Bugs's. The stuttering Bugs called, "In...In...Inj...Injuns!" as another arrow buried itself in Bugs's chest, showing only the quivering feathers of the fletching protruding from his ribcage.

Pops dove into the wagon, grabbing his rifle and another. The careless men had left the rifles in the wagon or the scabbards of their saddle, only Baker carried his at his side. Pops tossed a rifle to Skeeter and jacked a round into the chamber of his own rifle. He crawled under the seat and slowly lifted his head to find a target, just as the rest of the timber on both sides of the creek belched Sioux warriors, screaming, shooting, and charging the camp of the white men.

Baker dropped behind a rock that sat beside the creek

and willows, caught a glimpse of a warrior, and fired the
first shot of defense and dropped a screaming warrior.
The man in charge, experienced at battle, determined to
order the others around, had failed to shout a warning to
the others, but found cover for himself and fired the first
round. But screaming warriors coming from all about
them silenced the big man as he came to his knees, wide-
eyed, searching for a target. He cocked the hammer on
the Spencer repeater, pulled the trigger, but nothing
happened. He did it again with the same result and
continued cocking the hammer, aiming, pulling the
trigger and screaming, but his fear had made him forget
to drop the lever and jack another round into the
chamber and continued to think he was shooting when
nothing was happening. Two warriors charged, one with
a rifle, another with a lance and war shield. One jumped
atop the big rock, screamed his war cry into the face of
the big Baker, as the second warrior drove his lance into
his side. The big man rose to his feet, dropped his rifle
and grabbed at the lance, looking wide-eyed at the
warrior on the other end. The blast of the rifle in the
hands of the first warrior blackened his face with powder,
tore his jaw away, ripped out his neck, and blooded his
shoulders and chest as he fell backward, jerking the lance
from his side.

Pops found a target, a young warrior emerging from
the trees, bow at the ready with a nocked arrow, and the
old man dropped the hammer on the warrior, saw red
blossom on his chest and the hair pipe bone breastplate
shatter as the warrior was driven back, stumbling over
his own feet and falling to his back against a ponderosa
that stood tall and unmoving. The seasoned veteran of
the war jacked another round into his big Spencer,
cocked the hammer and searched for another target. He

spotted another warrior splashing across the creek, splitting the willows. Pops bore down on him, squeezed off his shot and the Spencer bucked and belched lead and smoke, the big .52-caliber slug slamming into the solar plexus of the warrior and smashing him back into the water, arms outstretched and splattering the water away from his body.

Skeeter had bellied down behind some willows and tried to hide, but held his Henry rifle at the ready, waiting to shoot any warrior that might discover his hidey-hole. Whitey lay under the wagon and was firing his Henry as fast as he could jack rounds into the weapon, dropping one warrior, then another, but the Sioux were proven warriors and two came from behind him, each one grabbing a boot and dragging the man from under the wagon as he was kicking and screaming. He was on his belly and could not roll over to get a shot at his captors as another warrior jumped on his back, one knee on each shoulder and with knife in hand, began to take the two-color scalp while Whitey screamed. When the scalp was free, the warrior reached around and slit Whitey's throat, ear to ear. He stood with scalp high and screamed his war cry, just as Pops spun around and shot him in the face with the big Spencer.

The roar of the Spencer startled the other warrior that dove for the brush to escape, but Pops fired again and again, dropping one of the retreating warriors by blasting his thigh in two, and killing the second as the big slug ripped through his back and carried a fist-sized chunk of bone and flesh from his chest

# CHAPTER 22

## BATTLE

Movement coming from the trees warned Running Rabbit and the Blackfeet. Four mounted Sioux warriors were coming from the trees but facing downstream of the Little Pipestone Creek that carried the runoff into the bigger valley with the road followed by the gold seekers. The Blackfeet were behind them and unseen, but the Sioux were bitter enemies of the Piikani and this was the land of the Blackfeet. The Sioux had to cross the land of the Crow to enter this homeland of the Blackfeet. Now the Piikani band of the Blackfeet had the advantage, six warriors including Prairie Flower to the four Sioux, but Running Rabbit was not aware of the rest of the raiding party of Sioux.

The Piikani chief motioned to his warriors to ready themselves and their weapons, and at his nod, they spread out and dug heels to the ribs of their mounts and charged into the four unsuspecting Sioux. But the Sioux were ready for battle, expecting to take the white men by surprise, and at the first sound of horses, the four warriors turned and jerked their mounts around to face the charge. Horses splashed through bogs, willows, creek bottom, and the enemies clashed in battle. War lances were lifted and thrown, arrows shot, and the few rifles roared almost simultaneously. As the combatants clashed, the battle seemed to rage forever, but the few moments that seemed like hours, were quickly over and three of the four Sioux were dead, one had fled. Two Piikani warriors were dead, and two were wounded. Two of the warriors dropped to the ground to deal the coup-de-grâce on their enemies. Running Rabbit slumped over the neck of his mount, an arrow protruding from his back, the fletching at his chest, and Prairie Flower clung to the mane of her horse, blood showing on her shoulder, where a passing Sioux had dealt a glancing blow with his tomahawk.

Running Rabbit looked at the remaining warriors, struggled to tell them to load the bodies of their dead to the horses, and they would start back to the camp of Morning Dove. But the sounds of battle came from below, rifle shots, war cries, and screams all bounced off the canyon walls, warning of the battle below. Running Rabbit motioned one of the warriors near, "Tall Bear, go, see who fights. We must get to the camp of Morning Dove, my woman needs care." The warrior known as Tall Bear nodded, ran to his mount, swung aboard, and took to the trees to make his scout of the valley below and the battle that was heard.

———

FROM THE TRAIL in the trees, Eli and Morning Dove saw the camp of the white gold hunters. Eli nodded, pointing with his chin, to Sioux warriors moving through the trees on the far side of the creek and roadway, working close to the gold seekers' camp. Eli looked at Morning Dove. "The bunch we're following will probably cross over and come at them from the uphill side, there." Eli and Morning Dove were in the trees directly opposite the dogleg bend of the Little Pipestone Creek where the roadway crossed the creek and continued to the northwest. The valley of the Pipestone pointed north to the place where the tribes gathered the red clay stone for their pipes.

Eli was torn, knowing that if they did anything to warn the gold seekers, the Sioux would come after them and there were about fifteen or sixteen warriors in their party. But he also wanted to warn Running Rabbit, for the Sioux and Blackfeet were longtime enemies. But with six warriors of the Blackfeet, and the two of them, they were still outnumbered two to one. As he deliberated, his choice was made for him when the screaming war cry of a warrior split the quiet of the timbered mountainside. More war cries as the Sioux came from the trees on both sides of the creek beside the wagon of the whites. Gunfire erupted and within seconds, the low valley showed a pale thin cloud of gun smoke, stirred by screams of agony and war cries, as the roar of gunfire echoed across the narrow vale.

Eli had already passed the Winchester to Morning Dove and with his Spencer in hand, the Colt shotgun in the scabbard under his right leg, he nodded, "Let's go!" The two big horses erupted from the trees, splashed across the boggy grasses and across the creek. They crashed through the willows, came up the rise below the roadway, and topped out on the roadway to see the attacking Sioux and the few white men defending their camp. Already there were bodies strewn about, both Natives and white men, but a quick glance showed three white men, two in the wagon, one nearby, still fighting to defend their camp.

Eli stopped, made a quick survey of the battleground to see one Sioux warrior stumbling toward the trees to the left or north, two or three were in the trees on the right, one with a rifle, two with bows, all firing at the wagon. The clatter of hooves and the scream of another caught Eli's attention as a Sioux warrior was riding all out, coming from the upper end of the coulee. As he sighted the battle, he turned to the trees, and within moments, the four warriors spilled from the trees to the roadway, almost running into Eli and Morning Dove. Eli fired his Spencer from his hip across the bow of the saddle, knocking one warrior from his mount to the ground, as the others lay low on their mounts and headed down the roadway to escape.

Eli called out to the gold seekers, "Hello the camp! We're friendly and we're comin' in! Don't shoot!" He turned to Morning Dove. "Get behind me, if they see another Native, they're liable to shoot!" She nodded and let Eli go before her, following close behind.

As they approached the wagon, Eli called out again, "You passed my camp earlier today. We came after we saw that Sioux raiding party." He paused, "Looks like you did alright for yourselves."

Pops slowly stood, holding his Spencer across his chest, looking skeptically at Eli. He leaned a little to the side, "That an Injun behind ya?" he asked.

"She is, but she's not Sioux, and she's with me. There will be some more coming down the draw there behind you pretty soon, but don't go shootin' at 'em, they're friends of ours."

"Din't think a white man could be friends with a Injun. How come you is?" asked Pops, glancing to Pence who was still in the bed of the wagon and Skeeter as he came from the willows, both still holding their rifles.

"When you travel this country very long, you either make friends or dig your own grave. I spent some time in the army at Fort Laramie, made friends with some, enemies of others."

"What were those that attacked us?" asked Skeeter, looking around at the bodies of Natives and his companions.

"They were the Sioux you were worried about after your friend did whatever he did to make 'em mad."

Pops frowned, "How'd you know about that?"

Eli shook his head, "You passed my camp about dawn this morning and you were all talking loud enough for anybody in these mountains to hear you. Don't you know sound carries in the morning quiet and the mountain air, especially when you're in a narrow canyon like this?"

"You don't say," remarked Pence, stepping closer to Pops in the wagon.

Pops saw movement over his shoulder, turned to see the other Natives on the narrow trail, and asked Eli, "That your friends comin'?" He motioned with the muzzle of his rifle up the trail.

Eli stood in his stirrups, looked to see the Blackfeet coming, turned to Morning Dove, "Looks like some are hurt, better go see."

Morning Dove nodded, pushed her big palomino past Rusty, and started up the trail at a canter. Eli looked about, "You lost some of your men, I suggest you bury them and get on your way. It's the practice of most Native people to come back for the bodies of their dead. It might be best if you weren't here."

Pops looked about, looked at Pence and Skeeter, "You the only ones left?" he asked, frowning.

"Reckon," answered Pence, "but we might oughta check to see." He looked around, looked at the grassy flats and boggy land, "This don't look to be too good a place to bury nobody. Maybe we should just put 'em in the wagon till we get some'ere's else."

Pops pursed his lips, glancing from Skeeter to Pence, nodded, "Yeah, prob'ly. I ain't too anxious to hang around here, fer sure."

"Take their horses too," suggested Eli, as he nudged Rusty to the trail to meet Morning Dove and the others.

————

"THEY WILL NEED MY CARE," stated Morning Dove, as she walked from the camp side by side with Eli. They had been two days in the camp since the fight with the Sioux and Morning Dove had tended the wounds of Running Rabbit and Prairie Flower. Those of the chief were from an arrow that pierced the muscle of his chest and his back, and a blow from a tomahawk to the side of his head. Prairie Flower had been struck with a tomahawk that broke her collar bone and cut the muscles in her shoulder. Both would take considerable care and time for healing, and it was the responsibility of family first. Two of the warriors had taken the bodies of their dead back to their village and would return for their chief and his woman. One other warrior, Kills Bear, had stayed behind with Morning Dove and the others. Morning Dove looked at Eli, "Will you come with me?"

Eli paused as they walked, took Morning Dove's hands in his own, "Your people will return for their chief, and I know you need to tend to your sister and her man, and it will take time. You know I am searching for my boys and the last word I had was they might be up Bear Gulch. It would be best for you to return to your people and depending on my search, perhaps I will be able to come to your village after I find them." He was torn with emotions for this woman before him and the need to fulfill his promise to his wife to find the boys and encourage them to return to their home. He had entertained the idea of making Morning Dove his wife, but when he gave himself time to really ponder the thought, there were doubts. He thought if it was what was the Lord's will for him and his life, there would be no doubts but only peace, at least that is what he had been taught in his younger years at his mother's knee.

"But you will not come back," she mumbled, dropping her eyes and looking to the ground.

"Morning Dove, if it is to be, I believe that God will make a way. We do not know what may happen in the days to come, and I have made a promise I must fulfill."

"But you asked me to wait for you, and now we are together, does that not mean something?"

"But you also must fulfill your purpose and take care of your sister and the chief, and that is something just like my promise, is it not?"

"Yes," she mumbled, and turned away from him. She started back to the camp, and without another look to Eli, she disappeared in the trees.

He shook his head, looked around the narrow valley and the thick trees behind him, remembering the scripture, Romans 12:2. *And be not conformed to this world: but be ye transformed by the renewing of your mind, that ye may prove what is that good, and acceptable, and perfect, will of God.* He lifted his head to look to the heavens and spoke softly, "You know, you could make it a little easier for us to understand, don'tchu think?"

# CHAPTER 23

## TRAVEL

He stood beside his big stallion as Rusty nudged him with his nose and watched Morning Dove as she fussed with Prairie Flower and Running Rabbit, helping them mount their horses, wincing for them as they flinched at the pain of movement. Six other warriors had come from their village to protect their chief and his woman as they sought to return to their village. He could tell by the way Tall Bear showed his attention to Morning Dove that he was one that had wanted her for his woman, but Morning Dove paid little heed to the warrior, giving all her attention to her sister and her man, the chief.

When the warriors of the Piikani and Morning Dove had begun to ready their animals for the return to their village, Eli had also readied his for the journey he faced to make it to Bear Gulch. Now he stood beside his horse, watching Morning Dove make the last of her preparations and thought she was fussing and fidgeting over nothing, probably stalling her departure because of Eli and what must be said with their parting. Eli moved closer and stood behind her as she adjusted the cinch on her saddle. She stepped back into his arms, twisting around to face him and embrace him, holding tight as if to never let him go, until Eli pushed back, holding her at arm's length to say his goodbye.

Morning Dove looked long into Eli's eyes, "I will pray to *Apistotoke* to guide you to your sons and for *Nah-too-si* to go with you for a good journey." She paused, cocking her head to the side, and added, "I will also ask for you to return, but if I do not see you after one more summer, I will wait no longer."

Eli nodded, "And I will pray that God will guide you and protect you and your people. I will ask for your safety and for you to know what is His plan for your life. If it is to be, He will bring us together in His time."

She pulled him close, hugged him tight and pulled away, looked deep into his eyes as if she was trying to see into his soul, and turned to mount her big palomino. She reached down and clasped his hand, lifted her head, and nudged the palomino to the lead of the group, dropping into the draw and up to the road, leading the band to the southeast without ever looking back.

Eli grinned, shook his head, and swung aboard his claybank stallion, tugged on the lead of the grey who had shrugged off his wounds and eagerly took to the trail on the heels of Rusty and Eli. The horses pushed through the tall grasses to cross the narrow draw, but Eli kept them on the trail that moved through the trees, the familiar route northwest that would take them to the trail at the mouth of the valley and into the flats beyond.

He gave Rusty his head and let him move at his own pace, the lead to the grey fell slack as the packhorse easily matched the pace of the stallion and Eli's mind took him on a journey of its own through the last few days together with Morning Dove. He thought of how he was tempted to take Morning Dove as his wife, thinking only of the company on his journeys and the pleasant way of the woman who tended to meet Eli's needs before he even realized. He smiled at the memory of the times she put a cup of coffee in his hands while he sat pondering the way of things, or how she made certain his blankets were ready and her attention to the horses. Although he had a fondness for her that bordered on love, he did not feel that way about her, and he had given a lot of thought to what it would be like for her whenever they were to be among whites and their prejudices. He remembered Chaplain Haney talking about II Corinthians 6:14, *"Be ye not unequally yoked together with unbelievers..."* that, he said, told of Christians wanting to marry someone that did not know the Lord as their Savior and were not Christians. He spoke of the hardships of the conflict as the rest of the verse talks about...*and what communion hath light with darkness.* Just like when Morning Dove spoke about the names of her gods and that she would pray to them, and how he had talked about praying for God's will. He had never talked to Morning Dove about the Bible and what it says about accepting Christ as savior, maybe that was his fault. If she had understood and chose to accept Christ, then they would not be believer and unbeliever.

He shook his head at the thought, realizing how easy it is to become so obsessed with the less important things and forget about eternal matters. Wasn't that the way of most people, focusing on the here and now and doing little planning for the hereafter? The sudden stop of Rusty brought his attention back to the present as he looked down to see Rusty's head lifted, ears pricked, and a low rumble in his chest together with a nervous stepping. Something was wrong, some perceived danger that stopped the stallion. Eli slowly moved, looking through the trees to the roadway on the far side of the little creek, the bottom of the coulee that held the thickets of willows and alders and scattered aspen. He stood in his stirrups and leaned to the side to look through a break in the tall spruce and saw movement.

Standing in a backwater of the little creek was a monstrous moose with its wide-panned antlers, the tips showing strips of hanging velvet. The bulbous nose moved as he chewed some fresh greenery from under the water and the dewlap dangling under his chin. The span of the antlers was easily the breadth of a man's reach, probably over five feet. The big bull stopped chewing, turned to look in the direction of Eli and the horses, and stood unmoving for several moments. Eli watched, not realizing he was holding his breath as he watched this massive spectacle of the wild, and then the bull resumed his harvesting of the lily roots. The moose had few predators, usually only the grizzly or a pack of wolves, but those attacks were few as the big bull was a formidable beast. And this bull was more than Eli could eat in a month, so he chose to pass it by in favor of a smaller mule deer or similar. He nudged Rusty and the stallion resumed his pace on the trail of the ancients.

Eli knew he had most of a week on the trail ahead of him, and after taking the extra time with the grey and the Sioux battle, he was behind schedule. He had hoped to get to Bear Gulch before midsummer, but that might not happen. It was nearing midday when the trail broke from the timber to show a long, wide fertile valley stretched out before him. Big, black-timbered mountains stood off his right shoulder and stretched out to the north, while rolling hills bordered the big valley on his left and beyond them in the far distance, shadowy mountains framed the land before him. A chuckling creek hid itself in the willows as it hugged the shoulder of the mountains that stretched long timbered fingers into the edge of the valley. Eli pushed Rusty to a likely looking rest stop among the aspen at the lower edge of the pines.

He had been told of the small mining camp settlement in the upper end of this valley, but he was well stocked and decided to bypass the settlement and save some time. With no word of the boys from Virginia City and west, he was not optimistic of any word from this little scattering of houses and a few businesses.

While he let Rusty and the grey graze on the grass in the clearing, Eli leaned back against the chalky white bark of a big aspen and sat down, stretching out his long legs and digging his watch from his pocket. He popped the cover open, saw it was just past twelve, and absentmindedly began to wind the gold pocket watch, a present from his father on his graduation from West Point, and let his mind travel through the halls of memories.

"Hello the camp! Got'ny coffee?" came the hail that stirred Eli awake. He was surprised he dozed in the shade, but the rude awakening brought a frown to his face as he looked to see a scruffy-looking old-timer astraddle a hammerheaded crowbait black horse and dragging a reluctant mule behind. "I ain't had no coffee since 'fore the war, seems like, an' I shore fancy me a cup!"

Eli flipped the tail of his jacket away from the holstered Colt .44, and answered, "There might be some left in the pot, welcome to it, long's you're friendly."

"Oh, I'm friendly sure 'nuff, too old to be anything

different!" declared the old-timer as he moved nearer the day camp. He looked to be just a little near the century mark, but up close the whiskers, wrinkles, and dirt betrayed his lesser years. Eli guessed him to be on the far side of fifty, which in the mountains and gold country was considered to be old.

He slid from his saddle, a remnant from the early part of the Civil War, the McClellan that was not a favorite of the cavalry. Eli nodded, motioned to the coffeepot and as the man poured himself a cup of the thick black brew, Eli asked, "You in the cavalry?"

"Hehehehe...you betcha! First Dragoons, Colonel Henry Dodge! I was with 'em since Jefferson Barracks!" The old man chuckled, lifted his coffee, and took a long draught, making Eli wince as he knew how hot the brew was and the old man chugged it down without hesitation. "Ummm, good coffee! Reminds me of th' Dragoons!" He refilled his cup, sat down on a rock, and with elbows on his knees, he looked at Eli, "You in the war?"

Eli grinned, nodded, "Yup," without elaborating.

"Wal, ya gonna tell me? Blue or grey?"

"Blue, Sheridan."

The old man squinted, twisted his moustache and he looked critically at Eli, "Yeah, you look like a horse soldier." He sipped his coffee, "Lookin' fer gold now, are ye?"

"Nope. Lookin' for muh stepsons, they run off an' their ma wanted 'em to come home. Heard they were lookin' for gold, so..." he shrugged.

"Big country to find two men among so many others doin' the same thing."

"Ummhmm."

"Ya goin' north?"

"Ummhmm."

"Care fer some comp'ny?"

"Mebbe," chuckled Eli, grinning at the man.

"Talkative cuss, ain'tcha," grumbled the old-timer. "I'm Tubbs, cuz I don't like gettin' in 'em an' I got one o' muh own," he grinned, patting his potbelly.

## CHAPTER 24

## SILVER BOW

"So, Eli, you be headed up north to Bear Gulch, is it?" questioned the old man, now known as Tubbs.

Eli stood, walked to the fire to pick up the almost empty coffeepot. He held it out to the man to offer the last of the coffee, and Tubbs gladly lifted his cup for a refill. Eli grinned at the man, filled his cup, and tossed the dregs out on the remains of the fire. He frowned as he asked, "Don't remember sayin' anythin' about Bear Gulch. Just headin' north."

"Wal, I figgered since Bear Gulch is the latest hot spot fer gold, that was where you was headin'. Am I right?"

Eli turned away to start for the packs to put away the coffeepot, threw the answer over his shoulder with, "Sounds reasonable. That where you're heading?"

"I thot it'd be as good as anyplace. I'se allus been game for pickin' up a few nuggets. Ain't much for all the work no more. Figger I found 'nuff to last the rest o' muh years."

Eli turned to look at the scruffy figure that didn't appear to have enough to last the week. "Either you hit it big or you don't plan on havin' many years left."

"Hehehehe…just so you don't git no idees, I done alright, and had 'nuff sense to put it in the bank. Don't need to be breakin' muh back packin' all them nuggets 'round."

"Well, that was smart. But why go to Bear Gulch?"

"Thot I might run into some o' muh old friends. Most o' those what struck it big cashed out an' headed back east to fam'ly, but a few of 'em are still scratchin' an' diggin', cain't never get 'nuff."

"Yeah, I know the type."

"So, we travelin' together?" asked Tubbs, as he struggled to stand, twisting and scrunching with groans and gripes, mumbling something about old age and joints.

Eli chuckled as he finished with the packs and saddles of his horses, turned to look at the old man, who stood, bow legged, with only two tobacco-stained teeth showing from his grinning mouth. "I reckon we can keep comp'ny a spell."

"Hehehe…" cackled Tubbs, as he went to his horse and mule, snatched up the reins, and grabbed the stirrup to climb aboard. As he swung into his saddle, he looked at Eli, who was now mounted, and bent to pick up the lead of the grey, "Lead on, young'un, I'll be right behin'ja!"

————

THE BIG BOWL lay before them, lush, green, wide, and long, framed by black-timbered mountains. The tall grasses stood high and brushed the bellies of the horses as Tubbs pulled beside Eli, he motioned to the north with a wide sweep of his arm, "Hear tell, 'tweren't nuthin' atall in this entire valley 'fore the war. They say ol' Lewis an' Clark came thru thisaway. Don't know 'bout that, but from what they say, there weren't no gold or nuthin' till the strike down Alder Gulch, an' 'bout that time fellers were scattered out nigh unto ever'where, diggin' into ever' hillside an' pannin' ever stream. That's when they started that little minin' camp yonder."

"You been through here before?" asked Eli.

"Been all o'er this country, panned most streams, dug into most o' the hills what showed promise, till I found a nice li'l pocket. After diggin' it out, cashin' out an' puttin' it in the bank, I just been moseyin' aroun' seein' the country, talkin' to folks."

"So, if you've been through here, I was told the best way was to head west-northwest through those mountains yonder, follow Silver Bow Creek to the Clark Fork and follow that north, then west into the mountains, to Bear Gulch. That sound 'bout right to you?" asked Eli.

"Yup, an' that'd be, oh mebbe, a week or so."

"So, if you've already been through here, why do you want comp'ny?"

"Hehehe…ain'tchu figgered out I'm a sociable cuss? I like talkin' with folks and gettin' acquainted, seein' new country, you know. And, well, I heerd 'bout them Sioux with Red Cloud an' how they's been kickin' up a dust ever'wheres an' well, all I got's is muh Spencer Carbine from the army, an' o' course muh Colt Army," he explained, as he slapped the holstered Colt on his hip.

"We had a run-in with some Sioux just a couple days ago," offered Eli.

"Wal, yuh musta done alright, you still got'cher hair!"

Eli chuckled, "Yup."

They rode in silence for most of an hour until they came to the banks of a meandering stream, lined with willows, alders, and cottonwoods. Tubbs reined up, stood in his stirrups, looking around, "This hyar is the Silver Bow Creek. It keeps on to the west into them mountains yonder," pointing to the timbered hills due west, "then cuts back to the north and it, along with some other little creeks, make the headwaters of the Clark Fork, that's the one whut was named after Clark, you know, the one with Meriwether Lewis that explored through this country nigh unto fifty year ago."

Eli looked around at the fertile green valley that spread out to the east and north. He glanced at the creek that chuckled over the rocks as it meandered through the valley and was no more than fifteen feet wide and appeared to be about a foot, maybe a little more, deep. He pointed to the opposite shore, "That looks to be a trail there," and nudged Rusty into the water. The horses paused for a drink, lifted their heads with water dripping from the muzzles and pushed on across the clear water to mount the far grassy bank and take to the trail.

Within a short distance, the timbered foothills shouldered in to narrow the creek bottom, barely offering enough of a shoulder to hold the trail. The two travelers stretched out single file, lifting cautious eyes to the steep-sided rocky butte off their right shoulder that towered over six hundred feet higher than the trail and almost all of it straight up. A few stubborn piñon clung tenaciously to a foothold in some crevice of rock, casting short shadows on the steep slope. Rocky outcroppings did little to hold back the loose talus that made long rockslides down steep chutes that left the trail littered with rocks, making travelers overly cautious with every step, afraid to make any noise that might loosen any teetering stones that could start another rockslide. As they rounded the shoulder where the little creek bent north, they were surprised to see the steep talus that was barren of green, showing only the steep slides of rocks that left the alluvial bend of the river more rock than sand. The trail mounted the rocks, prompting Eli and Tubbs to step down and lead the animals over the slide rock that littered the path and showed lichen and moss on the lee side of the rocks. The animals tiptoed across the obstacle course, heads bobbing and searching for footing, but once across, they lifted their heads to look up canyon, hopeful of no more rockslides.

It was a little more than two miles later when the hills receded, and the green valley opened before them. A long line of low mountains to the far north seemed to join the taller mountains on both the east and west and appeared as if fencing off the long valley. The sun was lowering in the west and painted a distant snowcapped mountain in shades of orange and red, sending lances of gold shooting into the western sky. Eli looked to Tubbs, motioned to the grassy slope on the west side of the creek, "Looks like a good place to make camp," he looked at the few cottonwoods that offered some cover and a bit of a windbreak; the water was clear and close and the grass plentiful. He nudged Rusty to the trees, stepped down, and began stripping the gear from both animals. A glance to the old-timer showed him doing the same beside a cluster of aspen saplings.

With coffeepot and coffee in hand, Eli walked to the grassy area, picked a spot for a fire, and sat down the bag of Arbuckles coffee beside the coffeepot and went in search of firewood. Tubbs gathered some stones for the fire ring, fetched some kindling, and started the fire with a lucifer and dry leaves. Within a short while, Eli had the frying pan sizzling with the last cuts of the cougar and Tubbs had prepared the coffee that was steaming its aroma from the little spout. The Dutch oven sat on some hot coals, others on its lid, and promised fresh cornbread biscuits. When all was ready, the two men had tin plates and cups in hand, Tubbs anxious to begin, when Eli said, "Let's give thanks first," he glanced to the old-timer and removed his hat, nodding to Tubbs to do the same.

"Our Father in Heaven, we are thankful for your many blessings, the safe journey, the good day, and now for our meal." He continued to offer thanks for all things, new friends included, and finished with an "Amen!" which Tubbs echoed as he put his hat back on and reached for a piece of cougar steak.

Eli grinned, waited for the man to finish filling his plate and cup and move aside, so Eli could fill his plate as well. Eli took a seat on the grass, legs crossed to hold his plate, and sat his cup aside, as he began eating.

Tubbs asked, "Did you say this was cougar meat?" continuing to chew as he spoke.

Eli chuckled, "That's right."

"Only had it onct afore, it be downright tasty, yessir. I heard other mountain men say they thought it was the best eatin' in the mountains."

"This is my first time eating cougar, well at least this cougar is the first I've eaten. Never thought I'd be eatin' cat, but my friend, Morning Dove, fixed it and got me to try it, and like you say, it is downright tasty."

"Wal, it is that. But I ain't never had it when it was prayed o'er. Reckon that'll make it taste better?"

chuckled Tubbs, reaching for another slice of steak from the frying pan.

"You tell me. I've never had it before, how's it compare?"

Tubbs frowned, looking at the glowing coals, shook his head slightly, and responded, almost in a whisper, "I do think it's better, whaddayaknow."

## CHAPTER 25

## INSPIRATION

Eli cleaned his plate, walked to the Dutch oven and selected another cornmeal biscuit and returned to his seat, using the biscuit to mop up any incidental tidbits of meat and gravy. He looked at Tubbs, "I take it you haven't done much praying." He had noticed how uncomfortable Tubbs seemed to be when he offered a prayer of thanksgiving before the meal.

"Huh, wal, I ain't no different'n other men. I did muh share of prayin' durin' the war. You know, when them cannons were boomin' and sendin' death through the ranks, and them southern sharpshooters pickin' off officers an' such. Tween tryin' to hold muh hoss from spookin' and duckin' bullets, yeah, I did me some prayin', but din't do no good!"

Eli chuckled, shook his head a little as he looked across the way to the old-timer who seemed to have a bottomless pit for a stomach. "I know what you mean. I come from a family that always went to church, made sure I was in church, even went to chapel when I was at West Point, but when the bullets were flying and I was praying, it seemed like the heavens were nothing more than a sounding brass. That was until I talked to a friend I met in the war, a Chaplain Haney." Eli paused, took a deep breath as he looked around, thinking about how to begin.

He looked up at Tubbs, "When you were praying, were you asking God to get you outta there, the battle, I mean?"

"Darn tootin' I was!"

"And here you are. Seems to me He answered your prayer."

Tubbs frowned, looked down at his plate and was silent for a moment, lifted his eyes to Eli, "Yeah, reckon so. Never thought of it like that. I guess I was thinkin' He oughta just get me outta the fight right quick like, but He got me through it instead of out of it. Hmmm."

"That's the way I was, although I thought I was alright, you know, church goin', religious, I kinda had what I called an 'ace up the sleeve' religion, whenever I needed it I could take it out, flash it around, and when I didn't need it, I could hide it away. But the chaplain told me that religion is man reaching up to God and faith is when we let God reach down to us." He saw the frown on Tubbs's face, and added, "let me try to explain."

"It's kinda like when we were in the army, we knew a lot of men, even knew them by their first names, maybe even knew where they were from, but that's about it. But when you know someone like a family member, a close friend, you know a lot about them and they know a lot about you, and you share things with one another. Now, until we have that kind of closeness with God, we're still strangers. That's why the chaplain told me we have to have a personal relationship, friendship if you will, with God and that begins with believing Him and taking Him at His word. And when we do that, we believe what He says in His word, the Bible. Understand?"

"Yes, and no. I understand what you're sayin', 'bout friendship, closeness and all, but I tried readin' that book, an' I couldn't understand it."

Eli grinned, "I know what you mean. That's because the Bible is God's love letter to His kids, and unless you're one of His, you won't understand it. If I showed you a letter from my wife that talked about what we did, where we lived, who we knew, it wouldn't mean anything to you, because you did not know her and at that time, you didn't know me. But, once you become a child of God, then you can better understand it. So, here's what you need to know..." Eli reached for the Bible that was in his saddlebags and pulled it out and began to leaf through the pages. "The chaplain explained to me, there are four things we need to know. First, here in Romans 3:10 and 23, it says we're all sinners." Eli grinned as he looked at Tubbs, "You understand that, don't you, that we're all sinners?"

"Hehehehe...I shore do, ain't no doubt I'se a sinner, yessir!"

"But here's the hard part, Romans 6:23 says the penalty or payment for our bein' sinners is death, and that's not just dying and going to the grave, that's death and hell forever!"

"Whooeee, but ain't there a way outta that?" asked Tubbs, frowning and getting a little antsy and squirming on his rock.

Eli grinned and nodded, "And that's the good part, you see here in Romans 5:8 it says, *But God commendeth* that's showed *His love toward us, in that, while we were yet sinners, Christ died for us.* See there, the penalty for our sin is death and hell, but Christ paid that penalty for us so we wouldn't have to, but..." he looked hard at Tubbs, "the rest of verse 23 in chapter 6 says *But the gift of God is eternal life through Jesus Christ our Lord*. So, since He paid the price for our sin, He also bought us a gift, that gift is eternal, or forever, life through Jesus Christ."

Eli stood, Bible in hand, and walked closer to the fire and sat on a rock beside the fire, to look across the firelight at Tubbs, "But here's what we have to do. It's not just believing that the gift is there, that'd be like you believing the cougar meat was in the pan, but what do you have to do before you get to taste that meat?"

"Uh, wal, I gotta get it outta the pan, onto my plate, and then into my mouth," drawled Tubbs, looking at Eli like he was daft.

"In other words, you have to accept it. You see, any gift is nothing and of no benefit to you until you accept it. I offered you the meat, the biscuits and such, but it didn't do you any good until you accepted it. Understand?"

"Yeah, now I do."

"And the gift of eternal life is the same. You can believe all about it, just like the meat in the pan, but until you accept it, it won't do you any good. Now, here in Romans chapter 10, verses 9 and 13, *That if thou shalt confess with thy mouth the Lord Jesus, and shalt believe in thine heart that God hath raised Him from the dead, thou shalt be saved. For whosoever shall call upon the name of the Lord shall be saved*. You see, Tubbs, to receive that gift, we have to believe in our hearts that Jesus paid for that gift when he died and was resurrected from the dead, and if we call upon Him, that's praying and asking for that gift, then we'll be saved from having to pay that penalty for our sins ourselves, and we'll have eternal life like Him, and spend eternity in Heaven."

Tubbs frowned, "You mean that's all there is to it? Just believe in our heart that he paid for our sins and accept that gift and its ours? Nuthin' else? We don't hafta get gooder an' gooder to get good 'nuff to get to Heaven?"

Eli chuckled, "That all. It has nothing to do with how good we get, Titus 3:5 says *Not by works of righteousness* that's our good works *which we have done, but according to His mercy He saved us.* See, Tubbs, if it was up to what we do, you know, good deeds and such, then we would need to know how many good deeds—ten, a hundred, a thousand? And if we could do enough, then when we get to Heaven, we'd be braggin' all over Heaven about how good we were. But it's not what we do, it's what He's done. And what He did was pay the price for the gift of eternal life, but...we do have to accept that gift. And we do that by calling on Him or asking in prayer. Understand?"

"Yup, I think I do. But what do I pray?"

"Tell you what, I'll pray, and we can pray together. I'll start, and if you mean it with your heart, you can say the prayer after me." He looked at Tubbs, awaiting a response and Tubbs nodded. They bowed their heads and Eli began with a simple thanksgiving, then continued with "Now, Tubbs, if you mean it, then repeat this prayer after me...Dear God, I want to trust you today...to take me to heaven when I die...forgive me of my sins...come into my life...give me that free gift of eternal life...and save me. Thank you for saving me. In Jesus name, Amen."

Eli lifted his head to see Tubbs smiling but with a tear streaming down his whiskery face and a light in his eyes as he reached out for Eli's hand to shake. "Thank you, thank you. I thought about that a lot an' never knew what I needed to do, or how to do it." He took a deep breath, let loose of Eli's hand, and looked at the dying fire, a slow smile splitting his face and parting his whiskers, "Yessir, I needed that fer a long time. An' I reckon I oughta be sayin' I'm sorry to the Lord for thinkin' all this time He didn't hear me, yet He did and got me safe outta that war and kept me in one piece." He shook his head, remembering the many times he faced death and finally realized that God had indeed delivered him to safety. "He musta done it for this very day." He sighed heavily, lifting his shoulders, shook his head, and said, "Yessir."

# CHAPTER 26

## BEAR GULCH

"Here, read it!" declared Joshua, dropping the letter on the chest of his brother, Jubal. He had been stretched out on his blankets in the shade of the big ponderosa with his hat over his face.

Jubal rolled to his side, pushing the paper away, and grumbled, "Just read it to me, I don't much care what you said."

Joshua picked up the strewn papers, shuffled them together and sat down on a nearby rock, elbows on his knees as he pushed back his hat and began to read aloud…

*Dear Mother,*

*I know it's been a long time since our last letter, and for that we are sorry. We have been on the move—we worked on a steamboat from St. Louis to Fort Benton, Montana Territory. Then we spent some time working as freighters between Benton and Helena, but we got the gold bug and decided to try for gold in the new discovery at Last Chance Gulch. We did get some, enough to keep us going for a while, but we got word that Pa was looking for us, so we left. With him being a career soldier, we knew he would not be happy with us deserting and would probably take us back or turn us in to the army, and Mother, desertion in time of war gets the death penalty so we could not take the risk.*

*We left Helena for a new strike at Beartown. We've worked for a packer name of Jimmy Smith, that runs a pack train of 200 mules up to the new strike. Since there's not a road yet, the only way to get their supplies is by packtrain. We made a couple friends, Comanche by birth but raised by a white rancher, and have worked with them on the train and prospecting. Jubal still thinks we can make it prospecting, but I think we'd be better doing something like packing or having a trading post or something. It seems the one's making the real money are those that provide goods and such for the miners.*

*We are thinking about heading further west. Jimmy says he could put in a word for us to work with packtrains that bring goods from the Columbia to Clark Fork, about a 350-mile trip with freighters and packtrains. We're trying to save money to do something worthwhile instead of working for others. Might even put in our own trading post or store. Also thinking about maybe going west to the Oregon Territory or Washington Territory. I think we could do some farming or ranching, maybe raise horses like the family did in Kentucky. This is a mighty big country and there's lots to see and do.*

*Will write again, soon. Don't know where you can send a letter that we can get, but if we land somewhere for a while, we'll let you know.*

*Love,*

*Jubal and Joshua*

"Yeah, I reckon that's alright. Long as Pa doesn't get a holt of it and come lookin' for us," drawled the sleepy Jubal.

"Now how's he gonna get a hold of it? He's out here

and she's back home!" growled Joshua, shaking his head in dismay at his brother.

"Wal, ya better get some sleep. Jimmy said we're headin' outta here at first light."

Their claim was the typical two-hundred-foot claim at the mouth of Cayuse Gulch, less than a mile northeast of Beartown, and had showed promise with the first few pans, but since their first week they had found less and less color and their hopes had dwindled with the color. Just yesterday, Black Eagle was the first to voice their disappointment, "Ain't getting' nuthin' but rocks and such! We make more money packin' for Jimmy in one trip than we're gettin' here in a week!" He tossed the pan away, stood, and stomped back to their lean-to, shaking his head all the while.

Two Moons, the usually silent one of the pair, looked after his partner, glanced to Jubal, and said, "I'm thinkin' he's right. This gold huntin' is more work than it's worth, don'tchu think?"

"It's lookin' that way. I know we've dug around, tried just about everywhere and gone as deep as four feet, but it's not too promisin', that's certain," replied Jubal, sitting back on his heels. "Now, the water in the creek has dwindled to its usual trickle since the last of the water has been let out of the pond." He spoke of the temporary reservoir dug by a handful of miners trying to improve the flow during the day. Although panning did not take a lot of water, those that had rocker boxes or sluices needed more to wash the ore and gain the paydirt. Water had become a major problem for all the placer claims with the only water coming from the high country with snowmelt and most of the snow had already disappeared. Many had talked about making bigger and better reservoirs in anticipation of the next winter's snowfall and runoff, but that would not help them fill their pokes now. That was the day before, now they had turned in for the night, frustrated but tired, and looking to make the trip with the packtrain back to the river and John Lehsou's trading post.

As Joshua stretched out on his blankets, put his hands behind his head, and looked through the thatched roof of their lean-to at the few stars, he said, "I think we oughta go ahead and pack our gear, look for somethin' better down below. Seems like every would-be miner in the north has come into this little canyon expecting to strike it rich—just too many of 'em!"

"Yeah, but we still hear about those that did strike it big, makin' the kinda strike that makes dreams come true!"

"Yeah, but I was talkin' to Joaquin at his store this mornin', and he knows this place like no other. He said the numbers are now over five thousand men up here and he's only heard of a handful really strikin' it big, and they were the first ones that came up here. So that figgers out to be about one in every seven, eight hundred that make any kinda strike that's worthwhile." Joshua chuckled, "And ol' Joaquin just laughed, and said, 'And I am making money off of every one of the five thousand!'"

"Reckon he is. We've spent money in his store, just like every other man here, and so has John Lehsou, down at the mouth of the canyon."

"Ummhmm, that's what I mean. The ones that are making the real money are those that are takin' it from the miners."

"Jimmy said Lehsou is thinkin' about sellin' his tradin' post," mulled Jubal, glancing to his brother, seeing the thin shaft of moonlight piercing the lean-to and painting his face.

Joshua turned to look at Jubal, "Maybe we oughta talk to him…"

"Yeah."

————

"Ain't that sumpin'?" asked Tubbs, leaning on the pommel of his saddle, arms crossed as he nodded to a house in the flats beyond. It was a big clapboard home, two stories, and appeared to have additional construction going on as well as other buildings nearby.

Eli frowned as he nodded, "Never expected to see something like that out here." He shaded his eyes as he looked at the sumptuous home. It sat back from the road, beyond a gateway with an overhead sign that said simply, *Welcome*. "What is it?"

"That's the home of Johnny Grant, he's the one what's responsible fer this whole valley bein' ranch country. Raises cattle and such. Got him a tradin' post there too. Them other buildin's have a livery, saloon, blacksmith, sawmill, flour mill, reg'lar town. Heard tell he talkin' 'bout sellin' out to a feller name o' Kohrs. Him an' his family's gonna be goin' back to Canada. He's a Métis. Folks say he had him more Injun wives than you could count. That was his way o' keepin' peace with the differn't tribes, marryin' into 'em. Got him a Bannock woman now, and some folks say he's got him nigh unto twenty-five chilluns. Hehehehe…"

"What's the town?" asked Eli, pointing with his chin to the settlement behind them.

"That there was called Cottonwood, now it's called Deer Lodge City. Ain't much, onliest is what it is cuz o' the gold strikes, doin' business with the miners."

Eli looked about at the wide expanse of green valley.

Flattop buttes stood to the left or west, backed by timber-covered mountains with granite tipped peaks that made up the western horizon, many miles distant. On his right, rolling sage-covered foothills rambled back to the south, with a frame of black-timbered hills beyond. Before them a jagged line of black-timber-spotted hills stood beckoning them onward. Eli glanced to the sun, just past midway, and looked to Tubbs, "We've got plenty of daylight, we should make it into those hills 'fore dark, ya reckon?"

"Hehehe...I know I can, as fer you on that crowbait plow horse you're ridin', dunno," The old man cackled, shaking his head at Eli and the long-legged claybank stallion that tossed his head at the insult. Eli grinned, shaking his head, and said, "Look who's talkin'. Dunno who's older, you or the horse!"

The trail sided the meandering creek, staying clear of the cottonwoods and shrubbery that held to the waterway, but the grassy flats kept the horses content as they grabbed a mouthful in passing ever so often, ambling at their own pace and covering ground as they passed through the valley. As they headed northbound, the bigger mountains lay to the west and the rolling hills to the east. By late afternoon the Deer Lodge Creek or Hell Gate River bent to the west and split the hills, pointing them into the timbered hills.

"Ain't too much further an' we'll be gettin' into what so many are callin' gold country an' after that, Hellgate Canyon."

The trail and river had turned westward, and the two riders watched the setting sun paint the bellies of the few remaining clouds with shades of gold, orange, and red, sending an occasional lance of gold skittering across the sky to paint a few random runaway clouds. The Little

Blackfoot River came from the northeast and emptied into the Clark Fork and appeared to push the river and the hills around the point of hills, but offered a campsite for the travelers where a little creek chuckled under some willows below the timbered shoulder of foothills from the south. Cottonwoods, alders, and willows shared the banks of the river and creek, offering shade, cover, and some shelter for the two men. They would camp and rest here, maybe for a day or more, before pushing on to Bear Gulch.

# Chapter 27

# Hellgate Canyon

"Well, Jimmy, I see you and the boys have made another good trip from the mountains. Plannin' on goin' into Hellgate are ya'?" asked John Lehsou, standing in front of his trading post/stage stop at the mouth of Bear Gulch.

"That's right, got some things the miners want sent out from town. Reckon Hellgate's the best place to get that done. You got some things to go or to bring back?" responded Jimmy. He had often taken the wagons of Lehsou to Hellgate or Deer Lodge for goods for the store, after making his trip up to Beartown with trade goods for the miners.

"I need you to take three wagons. Since Worden and Higgins built their sawmill and flour mill downstream of Hellgate, I kinda figgered that'd be the end of Hellgate. I got word they're closin' just about everthin', and if there's things that could be used up in Beartown, we can pick it up reasonable. Then I need you to go on down to the mills, they're callin' the new town Missoula Mills, and get a wagon load of lumber and one of flour. Sounds like Hellgate's gonna be a ghost town."

As he talked, two other men came from inside his business to stand on the stoop next to him. Jubal and the others had also come alongside Jimmy to listen to what Lehsou had to say. Jubal frowned, "Mr. Lehsou, I heard you were thinkin' 'bout sellin' out, is that true?"

Lehsou chuckled, looking from Jubal to one of the men at his side, "Well, Jubal, I've thought about it. My friend here, Charles Kroger, was talking about going up the gulch and see if we can't get in on some of the riches there. This other man," he stated, leaning forward to motion to the man standing beside Kroger, "who came up here with Kroger, is Conrad Kohrs, he's buyin' a ranch down to Deer Lodge and will be supplying Beartown and such with beef."

"Well, sir, if you're of a mind, my brother and I might be interested in buyin' your tradin' post. We got a little set aside, and if you could make terms agreeable, maybe we could work somethin' out," replied Jubal, glancing to his brother and back.

At the mention of a ranch, Black Eagle pushed forward, "And Mr. Kohrs," he began, stepping closer to the man on the end. Kohrs leaned against the rail, and answered, "Yes?"

"If you're startin' ranchin', my friend and I have more experience with cattle than with sluice boxes, and we'd sure admire a chance to get back to doin' what we know best."

"You're experienced, you say?"

"Yessir. We grew up on a ranch in Texas, helped Nelson Story with his drive up from Texas. Thought we'd try gold pannin' and done decided we'd rather be punchin' cows than crawlin' on our knees makin' mudpies at some crick."

"I'm headin' back to Deer Lodge shortly. I'd like to have you men join me and I'd be happy to put you to work."

Lehsou leaned forward, "How 'bout you and your brother goin' with Jimmy down to Missoula Mills and while you're gone, I'll think about it and decide if I'm ready and if you're the ones to take over. I might just put you to work here at the trading post, let you get used to how things are done, then decide."

"That would be fine, sir, yessir," answered Jubal, letting a wide grin split his face as he turned back to his brother who was also grinning.

————

JIMMY and his four-man crew finished de-rigging the pack mules and after a rubdown for each animal, they put them into the big pasture and went to Jimmy's camp. Black Eagle and Two Moons tightened the girths on their saddles, looked at the others and with firm handshakes and slaps on the arms, the two Comanche said their goodbyes. As they left, Jubal and Joshua turned to Jimmy, as Joshua asked, "So, what do you think, Jimmy, would it be a good deal for us to take over the trading post?"

Jimmy shrugged, "Fellas, I'm not one to be tied down any more'n I already am. If I had to spend the day shut up in a little cabin like that, I'd lose what little sense I have. But if that's alright with you two, and you can get a good deal, then…" he shrugged. After a long pause, he looked back to the boys, "But you gotta be careful with John, he's a purty smart fella and he always gets the better part of any business that he does. That's how he has done so well." He turned back to face the two, "But you got some time to think about it. We need to get them wagons ready, get on the move 'fore it gets dark so we can make it to a campsite I've used before. It's a good two days downriver to where we gotta go."

————

THE RATTLE of trace chains and the thunder of hooves brought Eli suddenly awake. The dim light of early morning struggled to show the grey skies beyond the trees, but the shout and crack of the whip told Eli that was a jehu aboard a stage making its run either to or from Hellgate. He did not know which stage line covered this route, but it was too early in the morning to be too concerned. He rolled from his blankets and with rifle in hand, he walked into the trees to greet the day and spend a little time with the Lord. When he returned, Tubbs had the coffee on and some bacon sizzling in the pan and the old-timer lifted a grinning whiskery face to look at Eli. "Mawnin'!" he declared. "Got us some breakfast goin'. Thot you might like to get back on the road to Beartown."

Eli chuckled, "You're right about that, but you're already soundin' like a doting wife. We had talked about layin' over here a day or so, but I was gettin' the itch to keep movin'. Didn't think you were in any hurry, though."

"Wal, I learnt a long time ago that ya' learn a mite more by watchin' an' listenin', and it was purty easy to figger you was a mite anxious to find them boys o' yourn. So..." he shrugged as he turned his attention back to the breakfast.

They were on the trail when the gold and pink of

sunrise painted their backs and the walls of the narrowing canyon. It was late afternoon when they stopped to watch a good-sized herd of elk pick their way across the bald slopes of the rolling hills to the north. Patches of black timber and the pale green of aspen offered respite and cover for the herd, but they were more interested in the tall grass for graze, and they kept moving as did the two men in the bottom of the widening valley.

Eli looked to the west as the valley opened like a broad fan, with the Clark Fork marked by the green cottonwoods riding the banks and waving in the breeze. The sun was lowering toward the mountains in the west, and it was time to find another camp. The lee side of a steep slope blanketed by tall fir, spruce, and ponderosa looked inviting, and they soon had a comfortable camp shaping up with the little fire sending its smoke into the widespread branches of the big ponderosa to dissipate into the darkening sky.

————

IT WAS late afternoon on the following day when Tubbs stood in his stirrups, pointed downstream, and said, "There she be! That's the ferry to Bear Gulch Station!"

"How much further farther to the town?" asked Eli, nudging Rusty alongside Tubbs and his hammerhead horse.

"Dunno, ain't never been there. Last time I was through hyar, weren't nuthin' up there!" He looked around some more and pointed down the river, "Them wagons mighta come from there, prob'ly goin' to Hellgate, it's another day or two downstream from hyar."

Eli gave a brief glance to the disappearing wagons,

turned back to the bobbing ferry and said, "Then let's get on over that ferry and find out just how far it is," said Eli, surprised at his own impatience.

Once across the river and back on dry land, the two men rode up to the trading post and stopped at the hitchrail. Two men were sitting on the porch, one appearing to be the trader with fly swatter that looked as much like a cat-o'-nine-tails whip than a weapon against pesky flying bugs. Eli shook his head as he grinned and leaned on the pommel of his saddle, pushed his hat back, and asked, "So, how much further farther up the gulch is the diggin's?"

The fly killer stood, leaned against the rail, and said, "You won't make it 'fore dark, but there's places you can roll your blankets out and build a fire."

"And then?"

"It's less'n half a day, maybe more. Only 'bout six mile, but it's a purty good climb all the way. The trail's not bad, long as you're not tryin' it with a wagon," answered John Lehsou. "Got plenty of supplies? They're all-fired expensive up there."

"Oh, we're just lookin' for now. But we have all we need. Thanks anyway," replied Eli, as he turned Rusty around and pointed back to the trail with a wave over his shoulder.

# CHAPTER 28

## BEARTOWN

The trail up Bear Gulch was through a narrow cut that split the steep rocky hillsides. With massive outcroppings of rock, scattered bunches of juniper, piñon, cedar, and a few random ponderosa, the steep hillsides seemed to loom above them as massive broad-shouldered giants leaning over the trail to intimidate all passersby. A short distance into the gulch, the timber changed to fir, spruce, and pine, bare patches painted with tall waving grasses and scattered aspen shaking their quaking leaves to greet the newcomers. Scrawny, white-barked aspen swayed with rough-barked cottonwoods, none reaching much height, along the now dry creek bed. Evidence of earlier spring runoff showed in piles of grey trunked logs, twisted and bent with the force of deep water, but now tangled and dry against rocky banks.

Eli led the way, his long-legged stallion stepping out and liking the climb. The trail had a couple switchbacks when it had to climb the face of a steep hill where the creek bottom crowded them out. They passed Tenmile

Creek that had no water and the fork turned slightly northeast. Long shadows crept through the trees as the arroyo grew dark, "I'd as soon keep goin', I think we can make it all the way. We've got some light of dusk that'll show us the way."

"You keep goin' an' I'll be follerin'. Don't make me no nevermind, muh horse can pick his way in the dark if'n he have to!" answered Tubbs, rocking to and fro in the slick-seated saddle.

"You keep slidin' back 'n forth like that, you'll get blisters on your butt!"

"Cain't! Already got calluses! Hehehehe…"

Prospect holes with their short tailings scarred the hillsides where unskilled and unknowing prospectors stuck in a shovel and started digging, hoping to find the gold of dreams, but found only disappointment and pushed on to the next likely looking spot to start all over. The creek bottom showed random signs of water, but not even a still pool could be found now. As they neared the site of Beartown, dark shadows of a few buildings lined out, backs against the steeper hillside, lights glowing from within.

Many men were moving about, shouting, gesticulating, and one stopped beside Eli's horse, "Miners' court, now, Pelletier's Saloon!"

Eli looked around, spotted the saloon next to Gee Lee's Wash House and a couple doors away from Joaquin Abascal's General Store. Eli turned around in his saddle to look at Tubbs, "Wanna go to the Miner's Court?"

"Shore! Ain't got nuthin' else to do! I ain't hungry or tired or thirsty or nuthin'…hehehe."

They pushed their mounts to the hitchrail and stepped down, slapped reins around the rail, and stepped up to the boardwalk. Men were crowding into the saloon and carried Eli and Tubbs with them. Although the saloon was already crowded, most moved about to find a chair or something to lean on allowing Eli and Tubbs to stand near the end of the long, rough-hewn timber that served as a bar counter. A bulbous nosed, potbellied, gruff-looking miner lifted a hand, pounded on the bar with the big pewter mug, and shouted to get everyone's attention.

"Alright! Quiet...Quiet! Miners' Court will come to order! Shut-up now!"

The crowd stilled, a low current of mumbles still moving about, but the man had the attention of most of the men. He stood on a chair, spoke loudly, and began, "Couple things ya need to know! The water will flow for two hours ever' mornin' beginnin' at seven! Then it'll be shut off so the reservoirs can fill up for the next day."

Someone from the crowd shouted, "We never voted on that! We used to get three hours!"

"Wasn't no call to vote. If there ain't no water, there ain't no water. When it's cut loose and quits, that's all we can do!" explained the speaker on the chair. "Now, there's sumpin' else. Listen up! We got reports of three men that are sellin' claims they don't own! They been takin' o'er claims when the owner's gone, write out a description of it, then find other newcomers that're lookin' fer claims, and sell 'em." He paused to let the others mumble about the news, then lifted his hands, "Now, listen. The three are said to be an old man with a ring o' white hair around a bald knob, average size, wrinkles, and a mite skinny." Some of the others laughed, and one said, "That sounds like most of us in here!"

The moderator continued, "The second one is younger, skinny, bug-eyed, brown hair. The last 'un is bigger, dirty blonde hair, square built. He seems to be the leader o' the bunch."

Eli frowned at the description, vague though it was, and remembered the survivors of the Sioux attack when he was with Morning Dove and her people. He knew little or nothing about the three, but knew the group had gotten into a pickle with the Sioux for something they did, and this might be their way of getting gold without the work, *if* it was the same three men.

The rest of the Miners' court dealt with minor complaints and suggestions, but nothing concrete was decided and the bar opened for drinks which ended the meeting. Tubbs asked,

"Any place to get sumpin' to eat?"

"Dunno, ask around. I'm gonna check on the horses and look around. I'll wait outside."

"Hehehe...I'll just have me a lil drink to wet muh whistle fer askin' aroun'."

They discovered the only possibility for a place to eat was a false-fronted tent café with a simple sign *Eats*. Eli pushed through the door, Tubbs close behind, and the two found a space on a long bench on the far side of an equally long rough-topped table. As soon as they sat down, a Chinese man wearing an apron poured them cups full of hot coffee, and asked, "You eat?"

"Yes, what'chu got?" answered Eli, but the man had already turned away and disappeared through a divider that separated the kitchen from the long tent dining room. Within seconds, the man returned with two plates full of beef, potatoes, carrots, and biscuits. He sat them down in front of the two, and said, "Four dollah!" and held out his hand for the money.

Eli chuckled, dug in his pocket for some coin, and dropped them into the man's hand. The man looked at the coins, looked at Eli, nodded and grinned as he turned around to leave, his pigtail flying behind him.

Tubbs shook his head, "Four dollars? Whooeee, I could eat mosta a month on four dollars!" He paused, looked at the plate, "But it do smell mighty fine!" and enthusiastically dug in, filling his mouth with several forks full, but did not slow a mite.

Eli shook his head as he chuckled, said a quiet prayer of thanks, and began to eat, enjoying the repast and looking around the crowded tent, searching for familiar faces, but seeing none. They soon finished and were hustled out to make way for other hungry men. They stood outside, looking up and down the street at the few buildings, many just like the café with false fronts and nothing more than a canvas tent behind. The main street was the only street, and the buildings were few, but more were underway. Eli spotted a livery near the end of the row and with a nod to Tubbs, the two grabbed the reins of their mounts and started walking to the Livery. Two ten-dollar gold pieces bought them board for the horses and themselves a space in the hayloft for four nights.

When they had the horses bedded down, gear stripped and stowed, the two rolled out their blankets in the hayloft. There were others already snoring and snorting, but they were glad to have a warm, dry place for the night. Tubbs looked at Eli, "You got you a pouch?"

"A pouch? What for?"

"I got some dust for ya'. You been payin' muh way an' I don't wanna owe nobody nuthin'. If you got a pouch, I'll pour you some dust."

"I don't have a pouch handy. I do have one with our gear. We'll take care of that tomorrow, but let's get some shut-eye for now."

"Suits me!" chuckled Tubbs, "Ya' gonna be askin' 'bout yore boys?"

"Yup. Most folks are more talkative in the mornin'. We'll check around the town first, and if nothing turns up, I might take a jaunt up some of the gulches, talk to some miners."

———

WHEN THEY CAME DOWN from the loft, the smithy was busy at his forge and anvil with some horseshoes and Eli waited until the man finished with one shoe before speaking. The smithy saw him waiting, put the tongs down, and turned to face Eli, "What'chu need?"

"Need some information if you don't mind," began Eli, digging in his pocket for the tintype of his boys. He handed it to the man, who squinted and held the tintype to the light that streamed in the front door, "Yeah?"

"Those are my sons. I'm lookin' for 'em, got a message from their ma. You seen 'em?"

The big man shook his head as he handed the tintype back to Eli, "Mister, if'n they ain't within ten feet o' me, I can't make 'em out. An' as far as havin' seen 'em, even if'n I did, I prob'ly wouldn't 'member. There's been so many comin' into this place in the last three months, they all begin to look the same. Somebody could ask me 'bout you at the lunch table today, an' the onliest reason I'd recomember anything 'bout you would be cuz you paid me in gold coin. Don't see that ver' often round here."

"Alright, thanks anyway. But I will probably need to go out into the hills, talk to some of the miners. What gulch would be the best to start with?"

The smithy chuckled as he picked up his tongs and

reached for another shoe, "There's Bear, Elk, Deep, Granite, First Chance, Melhorn, John Day, Shanghai, McGinnis, Cayuse an' a half dozen more. You got'cher work cut out for you, my friend. Good luck!"

Eli muttered a "Thanks," as he tucked away the tintype and joined Tubbs to make their way to the café for breakfast. Tubbs looked at his friend, "What'cha gonna do?"

"All I can do is keep askin'. Maybe I'll luck out and meet somebody in town and then decide." He shook his head as he walked, wondering about the twins with wanderlust

# CHAPTER 29

## CAYUSE

Tubbs walked with Eli as they beat the boardwalk on both sides of the single street. With no one admitting to seeing the boys so far, hopes were beginning to dim, but Eli stepped into the last store and probably the biggest, Joaquin Abascal's General Store. There were several men moving about, fingering the merchandise that was arrayed on long tables, hung from the walls and rafters, and stacked atop barrels and more. The big room was crowded with goods, but along one side, there were tables with men seated and playing cards, the light from the windows at their backs, and the men were enjoying free whiskey, compliments of Joaquin who kept a barrel of whiskey just for the card players.

The popular Castillian was standing behind the counter, tallying up a purchase for a miner, and Eli waited his turn. When he stepped up, he lay down a slip of paper with several items of supplies, flour, fruit, candles, and ammunition for his several weapons. The man looked up at Eli, grinned, and said, "I will fill this right away!" and started to turn, but Eli stopped him with, "First…" and dug out the tintype.

He lay it on the counter before Joaquin, and said, "Those are my sons. I had word they were coming here to Bear Gulch to try their luck, and I need to find them. Jubal and Joshua Paine. Have you seen them?"

Joaquin lifted the tintype, turning with his back to the light from the windows, and looked back at Eli, "You say you are their father?"

"That's right. I'm on a mission from their mother, she wanted me to find them and encourage them to come home, but she passed away before I could find them. Have you seen them?"

Joaquin squinted as he looked at Eli, "You don't look anything like them."

Eli grinned, "That's because they are my stepsons. Their mother was the wife of a friend who was killed and I promised to take care of her, so I married her before the twins were born."

"Ah, I see." He paused as he looked at the tintype again. He turned to face Eli, looked directly at him, and said, "I have seen them. What will you do with them?"

"Just talk. They don't know about their mother, and…" he shrugged.

"I know both Jubal and Joshua. They came into the store often. Joshua was here, uh, two, three days ago. He said they were taking the packtrain of Jimmy Smith. They have worked for him before. He also said they were probably leaving the goldfield."

Eli was astounded. After so many no's, he was startled to hear someone speak of his sons. He stammered as he asked, "Did they say where or when they were going?"

"Soon. Jimmy's train left early yesterday. But they did

not say where they would go. They had a claim with their friends up Deep Creek at the mouth of Cayuse Gulch, but they were giving up on it. I do not know if the others kept it or..."

"Yesterday? They were here yesterday?"

Joaquin chuckled, "No, the day before was when he was here, but they were going with Jimmy and his pack-train left early yesterday."

"Thank you, thank you!" declared Eli, putting the tintype away and starting to leave.

"But, I need to fill your order," responded Joaquin.

Eli chuckled, shaking his head and grinning, "Yes, yes please." He looked at Tubbs who was grinning like a cat that just caught a mouse, "Did you hear?"

"I did. Good for you! Happy fer ya'. What'chu gonna do now?"

"Dunno."

"Mebbe we should oughta go to that there claim, see if'n they tol' the others anythin' that might help."

"Yeah, good idea. We'll do that!" He turned back to Joaquin who had just set a stack of the goods on the counter, and Eli pulled out a twenty-dollar gold piece, "That should cover it. You finish filling it and we'll go get the packhorses." He turned away and started for the door without awaiting a response from the storekeeper.

---

IT WAS PUSHING on to midmorning when they rode through the one-street town, now amazingly quiet with all the miners back on their claims and busy at their work. With the water shortage, the camp had a rule for the men to remain sober during the week, a way to save water. The two men, with the town at their back, nudged the animals to the trail that headed east up Deep Creek to the gulch that was known as Cayuse Gulch. Tubbs asked, "So, how ya' gonna know which claim was theirs?"

"I'm hopin' there will still be others there. The store-keeper said there were four, my two boys and two others, all young men, that had the claim. He didn't know much about it, location and such, so we'll just have to ask around." He turned to look back at Tubbs, waved his arm around to indicate the hills about them, "There's no shortage of claims and prospectors to ask!"

The hills were either pockmarked with prospect holes or showed bare slopes with nothing but new stumps where the trees had been felled for building cabins or sluice boxes and flumes to carry the water to the claims.

The first claim they came to had two men busy at their rockers as the trickle of water chuckled through the rocks and over the small flume to splash the water into the rockers for the men to wash the soil free of the gold that would collect in the riffles. One man with the brim of his hat bent up, glanced up at the two men on horse-back and back to his work. "Whatever ya' want, we ain't got time to talk! Gotta wash while there's water!" and continued with the rocker. With a nod to the men, Eli nudged Rusty to keep moving on the trail.

Each claim was two hundred feet along the creek bed and side to side on the hillsides. There were claim mark-ers, cairns, stakes, poles and more, to distinguish each claim and every man looked with suspicion and distrust at the two men riding up the trail during the time the water flowed. Every claim had two or more men busy at work, some with shovels, drags, rockers, or pans. Each making good the time when the water flowed, the other work such as building flues, sluices, and such, could wait until the water shut down. Now was the time to wash gold.

Eli slipped his pocket watch out and flipped open the lid. It showed the time as 8:50 a.m., just a few minutes until the water would cease to flow. Eli nodded to a bit of a shoulder with tall ponderosa for shade and nudged Rusty into the clearing. The men stepped down, picketed the animals, and stretched out in the shade to bide their time until the miners might have time to talk. Within moments, Tubbs had his hat over his face and was snoring with such zest that Eli expected a bear to come from the woods looking for his mate. But Tubbs's mule ambled over, nibbled at the old man's whiskers and brought him full awake. He sat up, spitting and snorting as he looked at the mule who stood before him, head down, looking at him.

Eli chuckled, "He couldn't figger out what was makin' all the noise! I think he mighta thought you was a bear or sumpin'."

"Don't you believe it! That crazy mule just don't like me sleepin' when he cain't," growled the old-timer, struggling to his feet. He looked down at Eli, "Wal? We goin' to go talk to 'em?"

Eli chuckled, "Yeah, yeah." He flipped open his watch again, saw it to be a quarter after the hour, clicked it shut, and looked at Tubbs, "Reckon they'll listen now. The water's prob'ly done for the day." He stood and both men stepped aboard, turned their mounts to the trail, and headed for the next claim.

The claims butted up to one another, leaving no space between them and using every bit of ground that might possibly hold the stuff dreams are made of, at least that was the general thinking of the day. As they approached the next claim, Eli saw three men, two busy at building a sluice box and flues, the third digging and piling up ore at the head of the two rocker boxes that now sat idle. Eli hailed the camp, "Hello the camp! Can we talk?"

The man with the shovel stood, looked at the two visitors and with a glance to the others, he motioned them close. Eli spoke, "I'm Eli McCain, I'm looking for my twin stepsons and I heard they had a claim up this way." He reached into his pocket and brought out the tintype and held it out to the man, who said, "Step down, come on over."

Eli did as he was bidden and stepped closer to the man, extending the tintype. The man took it and looked at it, "What's their names?"

"Jubal and Joshua Paine."

The man frowned, "You said you was a McCain."

"Yup, they're my stepsons."

"Wal, they look familiar. I think I mighta saw 'em." He looked up as one of his partners came near and looked over his shoulder at the tintype.

"Yeah, I saw 'em. They have a claim up further. I think it's at the mouth of a gulch that comes down from the north hills. But I heard they was partners with a couple Injuns." Both the miners looked up at Eli, expecting some response.

"I don't know about their partners, although Joaquin at the store said they did have partners, all young men."

"Dunno 'bout that. Never talked to 'em. Been too busy. Waved at 'em when they rode past on the way to or from town, but that's 'bout all."

And so it went. They continued to stop and talk, some had seen them, none knew them, and Eli learned nothing new. After the last stop, Eli looked at Tubbs, shook his head, "I've never met a more suspicious bunch of unfriendly types. Reckon they're all thinkin' somebody's out to get their gold, if they have any."

"Wal, when all they think 'bout is gold and what they'll do with their riches, it don't make for right friendly neighbors. Can't blame 'em, not after what we heerd at the Miner's Court last night."

"Yeah, I suppose you're right. But..." he looked up the gulch and back to Tubbs, "We still haven't found the claim they had, and I'd like to find their partners and see what they know."

"If their partners are still there," mumbled Tubbs.

## CHAPTER 30

## CLAIM

E li and Tubbs took their time moving further up the creek bottom, ever watchful of things about them. "I'm gettin' that chill up my back, something's wrong somewhere?"

"You too? Thot that was just me...creepy ain't it?" answered Tubbs, as both men slipped thongs off the hammers of their pistols. Tubbs had his in a holster on his hip, out of sight under his jacket. They saw a stone cairn with a rusty tin can under the top rock and knew that marked the corner of a claim. Eli pulled to a stop, looked around, leaning on his pommel as he craned to look across the creek bottom through the willows and brush. He sat back, nodded to Tubbs, and nudged Rusty forward.

Three men were picking through things that lay scattered about. Two rocker boxes sat on their side, a shovel with a broken handle appeared to be cast aside, at the edge of the trees they could see a couple lean-tos. Eli reined up, leaned on the pommel, "Howdy fellas! What's all this about?" motioning to the scatterings around the site.

The nearest man, a tall square built man with a shock of blonde hair sticking out from under his Donegal cap, straightened up, one hand on his hip as he looked at the two uninvited men. "What's it to ya?" he growled.

"Oh, nothin' special. But since this is not your claim, it might be of interest to the Miner's Court down to Beartown!" explained Eli, his hand tucked under the fold of his coat, grasping the .44-caliber Colt Army pistol.

"What'chu mean by that? This is our claim!" he stated, glancing to a thin, lanky man that had come near, holding a rifle at his side. "Ain't this our claim, Skeeter?"

"That's right! This has been our claim right along, Pence. What're these two sayin'?"

"I think these might be the claim jumpers we heard about," declared the one called Pence. Their talk had brought the third man nearer, an older man that showed white hair above his ears, a wrinkled face, and squinty eyes.

Eli leaned forward, his left elbow on the pommel, the reins in his left hand. "What about you, Pops, what do you say?"

All three looked up at Eli, glanced to one another, the older man showing shock on his face.

Eli continued, "Since you fellas just arrived in this area this last week, how could this claim have been yours 'right along' like Skeeter there said?"

The big man began to stammer and stutter, looking to his partners for help, and growled as he looked back at Eli, "Who says we just came here last week? We been here right along like Skeeter says!"

The older man, Pops, spoke a mite softer, but loud enough to be heard. "You're right, mister. We just got here our own selves, but this claim was abandoned, and we took it over. We'll be filin' on it today. We didn't know who you was when we said that, now, we're right sorry 'bout that, but we ain't done nuthin' wrong."

Pence looked angry as he growled at the old man, "What're you sayin', Pops? You gonna get us in all kinda trouble talkin' like that. Now, tell him the truth, like we said!"

Pops looked at the bigger man, and said, "Instead o' gettin' all angry, Pence, you an' Skeeter there oughta be thankin' that man."

"Thankin' him? What fer?" asked Skeeter, glancing from Pops to Eli.

"Reckon you two have a mighty short memory. It was just a week or so ago that this man saved our scalps," answered Pops. "He's the one what came with them other Injuns and run off the rest o' them Sioux that wanted to kill us all."

Pence and Skeeter looked at Eli, back to Pops, and again to Eli. "Him? He was the one with the squaw and them other'n?" whined Skeeter.

"Ummhmm. If it weren't fer him, our scalps would be hangin' in the lodge o' some Sioux."

Eli chuckled, relaxed a little, and asked, "You say this was abandoned? Nobody around?"

"That's right. I heard a young man talkin' to the storekeeper 'bout leavin'. I asked him 'bout his claim, he tol' me where it was, and…" he shrugged.

"You plannin' on working this claim?"

"That's what we're thinkin'," answered Pops.

Eli leaned forward, "Then let me give you a bit of advice. Word's out on you three about you taking over claims and selling the rights to others. The miners aren't at all happy about it and they're lookin' for you three. If you're gonna be workin' this claim, you best file on it and keep your heads down till the other stuff blows over. Otherwise, you might find yourself stretchin' a piece of rope from a tall tree."

"But we ain't killed nobody," whined Skeeter.

Eli shook his head, "Don't matter. To miners, stealing a claim is worse than stealing a horse or killing a man. They'll get up a vigilance committee and hang you just as fast for that."

The three men looked at one another, and it appeared their bravado left them with shoulders sagging as they looked at one another and back to Eli. Pops said, "Reckon you mighta saved us again. We'll be doin' as you said. By the way, what's your name?"

"I'm Elijah McCain, and this claim belonged to my sons and their friends, but they did abandon it so..." he shrugged as he pulled Rusty's head around to leave.

Tubbs was close behind and moved up alongside Eli as they pointed to the trail again, "I shore din't expect that, no sirree. So you run into them varmints before, huh?"

"Yup," answered Eli. But before he could say anything else, the blast of a pistol bounced across the canyon, echoing its way down the gulch. Eli stopped Rusty, frowned, and looked upstream of the dry creek. The shot had come from the trees further up the trail. "That was a pistol shot, that's trouble," he declared, glancing back to the three men who also stood looking upstream.

Eli slipped the Colt from the holster and turned Rusty to the trail, letting him pick his way as Eli craned to see ahead. They had gone no more than fifty yards when they saw a donkey standing in the trail, head down, and what appeared to be a body lying on the trail. With a quick look around, Eli nudged the big stallion forward and pulled up beside the donkey and slipped to the ground beside the figure on the trail.

He glanced up to Tubbs, "Keep a look out, whoever shot him might still be around."

Eli went to one knee beside the old man, and leaned over, frowning as he felt for a pulse at the side of his neck. The old-timer groaned, opened his eyes to Eli and tried to pull away, but Eli said, "Easy old-timer, I'm friendly. Who are you and who did this?"

The old man groaned, fearfully looking about, "I…am Julian Guezala, and it was…Jack…Jack Varley. He beat me…robbed me of my twelve thousand dollars in gold. I thought he was my friend." He struggled for breath, grabbed at Eli, and tried to sit up, "He had a mask…I pulled it off and he got mad and beat me. I…thought…I was dead," he sagged in Eli's arms and lost consciousness.

Eli examined the man further, frowned, "He hasn't been shot, so what was the pistol shot about?"

"Dunno, but what we gonna do with him?" asked Tubbs.

Eli said, "You get his donkey, I'll put him on my horse with me and we'll take him into town. Maybe somebody there can take care of him."

———

IT WAS about a mile back to town and Eli and Tubbs stopped at the Livery, called out to the owner, "Hey Smithy!"

The big man came to the opening, frowned when he saw the old man in Eli's arms. Eli asked, "Where can we get him some help? He's been beaten and robbed."

"Why, that's Ol' Julian! Who done this?" growled the

smithy, coming closer. Before Eli could answer, the smithy pointed down the street, "Take him to One-Eyed Tom, he's a Chinee that's the closest we got to a doc. He's right next to Gee Lee's Wash house." The smithy looked to Tubbs, "You can leave his donkey here, I'll take care of him."

# CHAPTER 31

## VIGILANTES

When Eli reined up in front of One-Eyed Tom's, several men had gathered around, peppering Eli with questions. As they helped the old-timer down, Eli explained what had happened.

"Did Julian say who done it?" asked one man.

Eli nodded, "Yes, he said he pulled the man's mask down, recognized him as a friend named Jack Varley."

The crowd began to chatter, anger flaring, and Eli heard the word 'Vigilantes' and saw several men start along the street, talking to others and before long, a crowd of men, rifles in hand and horses in tow, had gathered near Eli. One man stepped to the front, facing Eli, "Since you brought him in, we need you to show us where it happened so we can find the man what done it."

"What are you planning on doing?"

"We'll get him, bring him into town for a trial."

"Alright. I'll go with you, it's not far." He stepped back aboard Rusty, looked at Tubbs, "How 'bout you taking our pack animals to the livery, wait for me there. I'll be back and we'll get us some dinner."

"Hehehe…I'm all fer that! Be waitin' on ya'," declared Tubbs, waving as Eli and the others started from town.

————

"Right there is where we found him. His donkey was standing with him, he was prone on the ground. He had been beaten pretty bad, we thought he had been shot because we heard a pistol shot, that's what brought us here," explained Eli. "He told me it was Jack Varley, said he pulled the mask off his face, that's what got the robber so mad. Said he got away with twelve thousand dollars in gold. He pointed up the canyon here," nodding to the creek bottom and to the northeast, "then he passed out."

One of the men had stepped down, examined the tracks, stood, and looked at the others, "That's what the tracks show, he took off thataway, horseback, an' in a hurry."

"Then let's go, men!" declared the leader of the posse. He looked at Eli, "You comin'?"

"Might as well see this through," mumbled Eli, slapping legs to Rusty to stay with the leader.

It was less than two miles to the confluence of Deep Creek and Gambler Creek, the main trail bending to the north and the tracks of the outlaw still digging deep as he turned up the north fork. The posse paused, the leader, an Irishman by the name of Murphy, directed two men to take the Gambler Creek draw, "He could swing around up yonder and come back down that way. Ain't no place for him to go further up, 'ceptin Top o' Deep. We'll stay on his tracks!"

The main bunch, a dozen strong with Eli, followed Murphy as the trail broke into the open as it split an old burn where grey skeletons of long-dead trees showed black on one side, grey on the uphill side, dead snags stretching into the barren sky. Just as the trail went into a gulch that was heavily timbered and unscarred by the old fire, Murphy called out, "Varley! Halt! You can't get away!" Eli came alongside the leader, saw a man standing beside his horse, both hands raised, waiting.

As the posse neared, Murphy said, "We're takin' you in, Varley. Old man Guezala done told us you done it! Where's the gold?"

Varley pointed to the bags tied behind his cantle, and at the direction of the waving pistol in Murphy's hands, he climbed back aboard the lathered horse. Eli had agreed to come with the posse just to be sure they brought the man back to town for trial, rather than hanging him from the nearest tree. When Varley mounted up and Murphy motioned to two of the men to follow him, Murphy and Eli led the way back to the trail on Deep Creek.

They had gone less than a mile when the posse met up with a man who was familiar to the others, as Eli heard several mumbles from behind them when Murphy greeted the lone rider, "Howdy, Deputy Pine."

"Murphy, men. Deputy Sheriff John Keene said I was to take custody of Varley."

Murphy chuckled, "Well, deputy. We planned on taking him down to Judge McElroy, let him stand trial, but since you and Keene want him, and you've already proven you can't get justice for anyone, much less keep a prisoner safe, I think we'll just keep him and take care of things ourselves." With a quick wave of his hand, Murphy shouted, "To the Top o' Deep!" The posse turned around and headed back up Deep Creek, leaving the deputy in the dust, but he turned back to Beartown, determined to raise a posse of his own.

Top o' Deep was a scattering of miners' cabins atop the knob at the head of Deep Creek. When the posse arrived, Murphy directed several of the men to set up a picket line while the rest, along with Eli and Varley, went into the cabin to barricade it in case of attack by the deputy and his followers. Eli looked around, knowing he was a stranger among a band of miners that considered one another friends, and asked Murphy, "What now?"

Murphy looked around, called one of the other men over, "Kelly, find McGhee, I got a job for you two." Kelly nodded, looked around the cabin and stepped outside, calling for McGhee, then the two men came back inside. Murphy looked at Eli, "The Vigilantes have some rules that we all abide by, especially when we're doing the business of the Vigilance Committee. One of those rules is: There must be a face-to-face identification of the outlaw by the victim. We can't carry out any sentence, no matter how guilty he may be, without that identification."

"So, Varley must be identified by the old-timer, Guezala?" asked Eli.

"That's right," agreed Murphy. He turned to the two men, "I want you two to go back into town, see if old man Guezala can come up here and make that identification. Do what you can, but remember, the deputy will try to keep you from getting him here, so keep your eyes open!" Kelly nodded, glanced to McGhee who also nodded, and the two men turned and left the house, took to their horses and disappeared through the trees.

Kelly and McGhee slipped into town, tethering their horses behind the livery, and walked behind the other buildings to make their way to One-Eyed Tom's. They

entered through the back and saw Guezala sitting on a
ladder-back chair, watching Tom brewing some tea. He
looked up as the two men came in, listened as Kelly
explained, "So, you see, we need you to identify Varley as
the man that attacked you and stole your gold 'fore we
can do anything. Think you can make it?"

"Not if I have to walk," answered the old-timer.

Kelly said, "You can take my horse, McGhee can get
you there."

"Then let's go! I wanna get muh gold back!" declared
the old-timer.

As the men rode from town, they were spotted by one
of the sheriff's posse men who sounded the alarm and
the deputy quickly set the posse on the trail of the two.
But McGhee spotted the posse, shouted to Guezala, "You
go ahead, I'll try to hold 'em off a while so you can make
it! Hurry!" The old-timer dug heels to the horse and took
off at an all-out run. McGhee saw him go, turned around,
and waited for the posse. He was surprised to see the
posse had been joined by the deputy from Cottonwood,
or Deer Lodge, Deputy John Keene. When they stopped,
McGhee spoke, "Howdy Deputy! What brings you to our
neck o' the woods?"

"You know durn well why I'm here. Where's the old
man?"

"What old man? I ain't an old man," declared
McGhee, trying to look confused.

"I want that man and the one that stole his money,
and I mean to have them!"

"And do what, Deputy? Everybody knows you and
your men can't keep track of a prisoner. Wasn't it just th'
other day when you ended up locked in your own jail and
some murderers went free?"

"Git outta my way!" growled the sheriff, digging

spurs into the ribs of his mount and pushing against the shoulder of McGhee's horse. He lifted a quirt to slap McGhee, but the Irish man grabbed it from his hand and slapped the deputy's horse on the rump, causing the big horse to break in the middle, put his head between his front feet and kick at the clouds with his hind feet. With two quick bucks, a twist in the air, and a sudden jolt when he drove both front feet into the ground, the deputy took flight over the horse's head and landed in a prickly pear patch. The deputy screamed for help and two men, stifling their laughter, went to give him a hand up, but kept their distance from the prickly thorns.

Guezala made good his getaway and rode into the clearing in front of the cabin at Top o' Deep. He reined up, climbed down, and was helped into the cabin to confront his attacker. When he entered, Murphy and Eli stood, motioned the old man to a chair. Murphy began, "Alright men, now begins the trial of Jack Varley, for the beating and robbery of Julian Guezala. Now, Varley, you were identified by Julian as the man that beat him. We tracked you from the place where the beating took place, and we found the twelve thousand dollars on your horse. You have anything to say?"

Varley said, "I'm innocent! I din't do nuthin'!" he declared, as a slow grin split his face. He sat with hands tied behind him and twisted to make himself comfortable on the hand-hewn chair. Murphy shook his head, looked to the old-timer, "Mr. Julian Guezala, is this the man that beat you, robbed you, and left you for dead?"

The old-timer looked from Murphy to Varley, "Why did you do it, Jack. I thought you were my friend?"

Varley dropped his head, mumbling something incoherent.

"So, Mr. Guezala, do you say this is the man?"

"Si, si, he is the man. He beat me and robbed me and left me for dead. If it was not for that man," pointing to Eli, "I would be dead already."

Murphy looked around at the men in the cabin, which included those from outside, and asked, "What do you men say? Is this man guilty or not guilty?"

With one voice, filled with anger, the men responded, "Guilty! Hang him!"

Murphy turned to Varley, shook his head, "You heard'em, Jack Varley. You will be hanged."

He was led from the cabin to a big ponderosa that stood close to a hundred feet high with big branches that spread wide. Someone had already thrown a rope over one of the big lower limbs that was about ten feet off the ground. The noose was put over Jack's head, tightened around his throat, and he was lifted to the back of a horse.

"Got anything to say Jack?" asked Murphy.

He looked around the group, "Anybody got a jug so I can have some whiskey?"

One man stepped forward, motioned to a big man to come near, and was lifted up so he could give Varley a good draught from the jug. Varley grinned as the jug was taken away and the man lowered to the ground. Dribbles came from Varley's smiling mouth, and with a "Thanks fellas," he kicked the horse out from under him and swung from the big limb that bobbed overhead. Varley's feet barely cleared the ground as he kicked about, but soon hung still. The crowd was silent, and the men began to disburse.

Eli walked silently to his horse, stepped aboard, and started back to town.

# CHAPTER 32

## DIRECTION

"Sorry, Jimmy, you ain't gonna find much, if anything, hereabouts," said Jerome Shockley. "I'm just here with those two fellas to get the rest of the records from the county seat. They moved that to Missoula Mills, too, and the only things left ain't even worth pickin' up! Since muh Uncle P.J. committed suicide, his boardin' house was the last to close and ain't nuthin' there worth gettin'."

Jimmy and his helpers, Jubal and Joshua, stood together looking around the beginnings of the ghost town previously known as Hellgate. Shockley had turned away to finish packing the rest of the things from the county seat. Jubal looked at Jimmy, "It looks like everything's been cleaned out alright, reckon we'd best move on and make it to Missoula Mills 'fore dark."

"Yeah, you're right about that." Jimmy took one last look around and started walking back to the wagons. The brothers walked beside him in the middle of what had been the main street of the town, now nothing but tracks of other wagons that had hauled everything from the once bustling little settlement. Jimmy voiced his memories of the town a bit wistfully. "When Woodward and Clements built their new store, folks were excited about the town growing. I thought I might quit doin' the pack-train and settle down here. I think the news of the last of the Plummer Gang gettin' hung mighta scared off some of the businesses and families, that sort of thing scares folks. Don't know why, after they been caught an' hung ain't nuthin' to be scared of then, they're dead!" he declared, kicking aside a tumbleweed that was bouncing down the dusty street. "I remember, couple years back, when they even hung the son of a chief of the Pend d'Oreilles. I reckon there were quite a few hangin's in this town." He chuckled at the memory and reached out to stroke the neck of the lead team of his wagon. He looked at the brothers, "Well, follow me, we'll go to the new mills downriver."

As the three wagons were pulling into the new settlement, Jimmy spotted the two mills beside the river and drove the team to pull up near what appeared to be a loading dock beside the mill. A man standing on the platform waved, "Howdy, Jimmy! You here for some flour for Lehsou?" Jimmy recognized the man as Frank Worden, one of the owners of the mill.

Jimmy grinned, nodded, "And myself," he hollered. "Got three wagons here, need flour and lumber to fill at least two of 'em!" declared Jimmy, wrapping the lines around the long brake handle and stepping down.

"Good, good. C'mon in and we'll get started with the flour."

Jimmy's feet had barely touched ground when a ruckus nearer the settlement caught their attention. Jimmy frowned as he saw several horses, some saddled, others with harness, all with reins and more dragging, were stampeding from the town. Jimmy looked to Worden, "What's that about?"

Worden stood with hands on hips, laughing at the sight, "Ah, that's probably from that camel packtrain of Sammy Hilger, the horses and mules stampede at the sight of 'em! Every time!" he chuckled as he turned away to go into the mill to begin sorting bags and more for Jimmy. As the two men busied themselves with the several bags, Jimmy asked, "You say that happens every time?"

Worden chuckled, "Yup, and if'n you wanna learn some new curse words, all you need to do is be in town when the horses stampede! You never heard the like," he chuckled. "But every time I see 'em, I can't help but remember a happenin' that took place somewhere 'tween here an' Helena. Seems there was a fella out west here on a huntin' trip, saw the camels grazin' in a field, thought they was moose!" he laughed at the memory. "Wal, he snuck up on the hill, took careful aim, pulled the trigger, and killed one! But the owner was nearby and came runnin', shoutin' and screamin' and lettin' loose with some o' those new curse words. The hunter, fella name of McNear, told him to back off and be still and he'd get another one o' them moose!"

Worden stepped back and took out a pipe, stuffed it as he chuckled, and struck a lucifer to light up, puffed a cloud of smoke and continued. "When he realized they were camels instead o' moose, he told Sammy, 'Wal, if that's what it is, you can have it.' But Sammy compelled the shooter McNear to give up his gun, ammunition, watch, and all the money he had, plus sign over a deed to a claim McNear owned in Ophir Gulch. Then Sammy made him dig a grave and bury the camel!" Worden laughed so hard his belly bounced under the flour-dusted apron. "After that, everybody call the shooter, 'Camel' McNear!"

"And he's still packin' those camels?" asked Jimmy.

Worden nodded his head, chuckling as he thought about it, "Yup, he packs goods from Walla Walla to here and beyond. Takes stuff all the way to Helena. Those six camels can haul 'bout the same as the packtrain I used when I came from Walla Walla, and that took seventy-six mules!"

"You don't say," answered Jimmy, somewhat incredulous.

Jubal and Joshua stood at the loading dock, listening to Worden tell his story and laughing as they hefted bags of flour and dropped them into the wagons. When they finished with the flour, Worden directed them to the sawmill, and they moved the wagons further downstream to side the sawmill. Captain Higgins recognized Jimmy and hailed him, waved him to the end of the mill building and came near to talk about the order for the lumber.

It was midafternoon when the wagons were loaded, and Jimmy suggested, "Let's take 'em to the livery, park the wagons and put up the mules, and get us a real meal at the café Captain Higgins told me about. We can put up in the boardin'house, get an early start, and be back in Bear Gulch in a couple days."

———

THE CAFÉ WAS popular and crowded when Jimmy and the twins stepped in, looking around for a place to sit. Jimmy was surprised when a man waved, and called, "Jimmy! Over here, Jimmy!" Jimmy grinned, nodded, and spoke to the twins, "That's a packer friend of mine, Six!" and started to the long table where the man sat.

Six said, "Have a seat, Jimmy!" motioning to the long bench across the table.

Jimmy nodded, motioned to the twins to sit as well, and as he took a seat he shook hands with Six. "So, what have you been up to, Six?" asked Jimmy, "Oh, these fellas work with me. That's Jubal and Joshua."

Six reached out to shake hands with the twins and they saw why the man was called Six. He had six fingers on his right hand and that made a handful when they shook hands. Six grinned, having seen that reaction many times, but looked back to Jimmy. "I'm still packin'. Just brought in a pack from up at Cabinet on the Clark Fork. There's a couple riverboats up there now and they've been bringing in considerable loads. I'm 'bout to trade muh mules for some wagons, make the trip easier, and then I can do the Mullan Road to Walla Walla."

"Now you're thinkin' big," replied Jimmy.

A woman leaned between him and the twins, setting tableware before them. She said, "Help yourselves," nodding to the bowls and platters in the middle of the table. "If you need more, just holler. I'll be right back with more biscuits."

Jubal smiled at the woman, "Thank you, ma'am."

She frowned, "I'm not a ma'am, I'm a miss!" and stormed away. Jubal watched her leave and looked at Joshua, "I thought she was old 'nuff to be a wife, that's why I called her ma'am," he shrugged, grinning.

The twins were hungry but curious as well, and when Jimmy and Six talked about riverboats, they paid attention. At a lull in the conversation, Jubal asked Six, "The riverboats, they new?"

"Yup, shallow draft, good steam power, haul a lot.

The captain was tellin' me they've had trouble getting and keeping crew, though. Seems whoever joins the crew, soon leaves for the goldfields."

Jubal chuckled, "We understand that. We crewed a boat up the Missouri, left to haul freight, then went to the goldfields. Now we're backtrackin' a bit."

"Backtrackin'?" asked Six.

Jubal looked at Jimmy, then to Six, "Yeah, we're leavin' the goldfield, thinkin' about headin' further west, maybe Washington or Oregon Territory."

Six nodded, "If you're lookin' for work, I can put you to work with me. You heard what I'm doin' and that'll get you further west than you are now, that is if Jimmy will let you go." He looked at his friend who was busy filling his plate.

Jimmy looked to Six, "And how am I gonna get three wagons back to Bear Gulch? I can't drive all three," he declared.

"Tell you what, Jimmy, I've got two men, maybe three, that have the itch for the goldfields, but I made 'em promise to stick with me. How 'bout we just trade? That'll give you drivers, and I'll have a couple men that will at least get me back with my load."

Jimmy looked at Six, turned to look at Jubal and Joshua, "That what you boys want?"

Jubal turned to Joshua who was grinning and nodding, back to Jimmy, "Sounds good to us, Jimmy!

## CHAPTER 33

## CLOSE

"While you was off gallivantin' wit' them vigilantes, I run into a couple ol' friends!" declared Tubbs, looking at Eli across the table where they were eating in the exclusive café called *Eats.*

Eli looked at the old-timer, frowned, "So, what're you gonna do?"

"Wal, they asked me to lend a hand with their claim, said they need a 'experienced' miner to show 'em what fer. Hehehe..." he chuckled. "They been doin' it 'bout as long as me, but I just done it a mite better, so I reckon that makes me a 'professional'!"

Eli dropped his eyes to his plate, "I kinda lost my appetite for this place anyway. I think I'll be pullin' out at first light. Think I might catch up to muh boys down to Hellgate or thereabouts."

"Wal, Eli. It's been all-fired good travelin' wit'chu. I do hope you find yore boys, yessir. And..." he paused as he dropped his eyes to his plate, then back up to Eli, "... I'm mighty grateful for what you told me 'bout Heaven an' all. So, I'm thinkin' we might be partin' comp'ny hereabouts, but one day..." he pointed up and lifted his eyes, "...one day, we'll be shakin' hands and shoutin' up yonder." He grinned with a grin that split his face and filled his eyes with joy and tears as he reached across the table to shake hands with his friend.

———

THE SUN WAS at his back when he took the trail west after leaving Bear Gulch. The sky was clear and a brilliant cobalt blue, the morning was already warm and the breeze that followed the river brought the smell of pine, cedar, and the dusty, almost crisp, smell of aspen. Eli stood in his stirrups, letting Rusty keep his pace, and lifted his head to the air of the wilderness, letting a grin of freedom split his face and filled his lungs with the wondrous clear mountain air. He dropped into his saddle, looked at the meandering Hellgate or Clark Fork River lined with cottonwoods, aspen, willows, and more. He lifted his eyes to the rolling hills to the north and south, those on the north or his right, dotted with ponderosa and juniper, the bigger hills before him that sided the river stood tall, clinging to their capes of black timber. It was beautiful country, and even with all its majesty, it still held violence and turmoil within its breast. He breathed heavy, settled into his saddle, and let Rusty have his head and pick his own pace.

It was approaching dusk when he rode into the settlement of Hellgate, and the emptiness covered him like a mournful blanket. Although he had never been to the town before, he had heard much about it, but what lay before him was the newfound corpse of a once living town. Dust devils danced in the street, dark windows glared with blank stares, shutters rattled, doors stood agape in awe of the visitor. Whispers of the past moaned through the already decaying structures, two buzzards perched on the top of a false front that marked the last of *Woodward and Clements General Store*, the paint already peeling from the sign.

Rusty and the grey were skittish as they looked from side to side, uncertain steps that matched their pace and bobbing heads and occasional snorts of hesitation. Eli leaned down to stroke the big stallion's neck, "It's alright, boy, easy now, we'll move on." He sat back tall in the saddle and nudged the big stallion past the squeaking doors of the empty livery and blacksmith shop with a sign *Buckhouse Livery.*

With the ghost town of Hellgate behind them, the horses settled down and quickened their pace as if they knew they would soon be stopping and getting some graze and water. Missoula Mills was a short way, but Eli nudged the big horse into the trees where the river took a big bend to the north and back again, offering a wide peninsula of graze and cover of big pine for a place to camp for the night. Both Eli and the horses seemed to relax as he reined up at the edge of a small clearing, the chuckling of the river heard through the willows and cottonwoods at the riverbank.

———

ELI RODE into town with the first grey light of early morning. He passed the mills, spotted a livery and a man, probably the smithy, pushing open the big door to begin his work for the day. Eli reined up behind the man, "Morning!"

The big man turned to look, frowned, "Yup, it is. What'chu need?"

"Wonderin' if you've seen a couple young men," he leaned forward, extending his hand with the tintype. The man looked at him, dubious of his purpose, but accepted the tintype, looked up at the man.

"What'chu wan' 'em fer?"

Eli grinned, "They're my stepsons. I'm on a mission for their mother. She wants to see 'em."

"I ain't seen 'em, but...there was a fella left three wagons here a couple days ago, there was a couple men with him, but I never got a look at 'em. Coulda been..." he shrugged.

"Where'd they go?"

"Dunno, I din't see, I was busy at muh forge. They left yestiddy mornin' early."

Eli reached for the tintype, put it away, and said, "Thanks."

He reined around, went to the café and stepped down to slap the reins and lead to the hitchrail and stepped up on the boardwalk, looked around, and pushed through the door. Several of the tables were occupied, but there was an empty table for four by the front window and Eli seated himself. A buxom woman came with a pot of coffee and some cups in her hand, she sat one cup on the table, poured it full, and looked at Eli, a question on her face. "Ya eatin'?"

"Yes, ma'am."

Without another word, the woman nodded, turned away, and poured several more cups full on her way back to the kitchen. She soon returned; arms full. She sat a platter of bacon and eggs before him, a plate of biscuits, a plate of thin-sliced steak and beans, and looked at Eli, "Anything else?"

Eli grinned, eyebrows lifted, and looked at the woman, "That's a lot of food!"

"Yeah, well, most workin' men are hungry. Eat what'chu can, leave the rest. It won't be wasted."

"Ma'am, could I ask you a question, please?"

She frowned, turned to face him, "Well?"

Eli handed her the tintype, asked, "Seen 'em?"

"Why you lookin'?"

"They're my stepsons."

"Saw 'em couple nights ago, mebbe more, hard to tell. Heard 'em talkin' to a packer who offered 'em a job packin' an' freightin'."

Eli grinned, "Do you remember his name or where he worked out of?"

"Nope, but I can tell you I heard him talk 'bout Walla Walla and Cabinet on the Clark Fork. Oh, and all I can tell you 'bout the man, he had six fingers." She frowned at Eli, "Anythin' else?" as she handed him the tintype.

"No, thank you. That's a big help."

She nodded and hurried on her way.

After breakfast, he asked around. Talking to the smithy again, the man at the mill, a couple merchants that might use a packtrain, but the only thing he learned was the man's name was Six and he had been running a packtrain for about three years. Most of the time he hauled from Walla Walla to Deer Lodge and Helena, but recently he had been picking up loads from other places. A wheelwright on the west end of town said he remembered Six asking about freight wagons but knew little else.

Eli thought of it, knew the Clark Fork flowed north into lake Pend d'Orielle and from what he learned, the Cabinet Rapids were the furthest any riverboat could come upstream. But Walla Walla was due west, and it was a longer journey but the Mullan Road led to the growing town that was also a hub for shipping supplies to the east or the goldfields of Montana Territory. Eli sat, somewhat dejected and disappointed, on the edge of the boardwalk, looking at the face of his big stallion, and he asked, "Well, Rusty, which way do we go? North up the Clark Fork, or west to Walla Walla?"

Rusty snorted and bobbed his head and stretched out for Eli to rub his face. "You're no help. Maybe I shoulda asked Grey." He stroked the face of the claybank, rubbed behind his ears and glanced over to a jealous Grey. He grinned and chuckled, "What about it, Grey. North or west? Whichever way we go, if it's the wrong way, it's a long way to backtrack and start over."

The grey snorted, bobbed his head, and stretched out for some attention. Eli stood, reached for the grey's face, and dug in his pocket for a coin. He fingered the ten-dollar gold piece, looked at it, and shook his head. *Now it's come down to a flip of the coin.* He shook his head, flipped the coin in the air, *Heads it's north, tails it's west.* He caught the coin, looked at the image, shook his head, and chuckled as he put it away. He stood, looked at the horses, "Well, boys, one thing for certain, we ain't gonna find 'em here!" He stepped aboard and nudged the big stallion to the road, anxious to put towns and people behind him, hopeful for the future as he muttered a short prayer for the Lord's direction and the journey before him.

# A Look at: Stonecroft Saga
## Volume One

**BEST-SELLING AUTHOR B.N. RUNDELL TAKES YOU ON AN EPIC JOURNEY THROUGH THE OLD WEST IN THIS ACTION-PACKED 5-BOOK WESTERN COLLECTION.**

After a bloody duel leaves one man dead, Gabriel Stonecroft along with his life-long friend, Ezra, are determined to leave town. A journey to the far wilderness of the west would soon begin.

One man from prominent social standing, the other with a life of practical experience, are soon joined in life building adventures.

*"A fun fast paced book. Perfect for the outdoors history loving reader."* – **John Theo Jr., author of the Brandon Hall Mysteries.**

Danger, excitement and never-ending adventure will follow the two friends as they face bounty hunters, river pirates and renegade Indians. With every turn they meet a new hurdle and just when they think they're on their way into the uncharted wilderness, they are faced with a new challenge, the like of which they never imagined.

*Stonecroft Saga Volume One includes: Escape to Exile, Discovery of Destiny, Westward the Wilderness, Moonlight and Mountains and Raiders of the Rockies.*

***AVAILABLE NOW***

# About the Author

Born and raised in Colorado into a family of ranchers and cowboys, **B.N. Rundell** is the youngest of seven sons. Juggling bull riding, skiing, and high school, graduation was a launching pad for a hitch in the Army Paratroopers. After the army, he finished his college education in Springfield, MO, and together with his wife and growing family, entered the ministry as a Baptist preacher.

Together, B.N. and Dawn raised four girls that are now married and have made them proud grandparents. With many years as a successful pastor and educator, he retired from the ministry and followed in the footsteps of his entrepreneurial father and started a successful insurance agency, which is now in the hands of his trusted nephew. He has also been a successful audiobook narrator and has recorded many books for several award-winning authors. Now finally realizing his life-long dream, B.N. has turned his efforts to writing a variety of books, from children's picture books and young adult adventure books, to the historical fiction and western genres which are his first love.